Olabooks International

http://www.olabooksinternationalselfpub.com

ISBN: 978-1-7353671-4-9

Cover Photo 2020www.gettyimages.com. All rights reserved-used with permission.

PRINTED IN THE UNITED STATES OF AMERICA

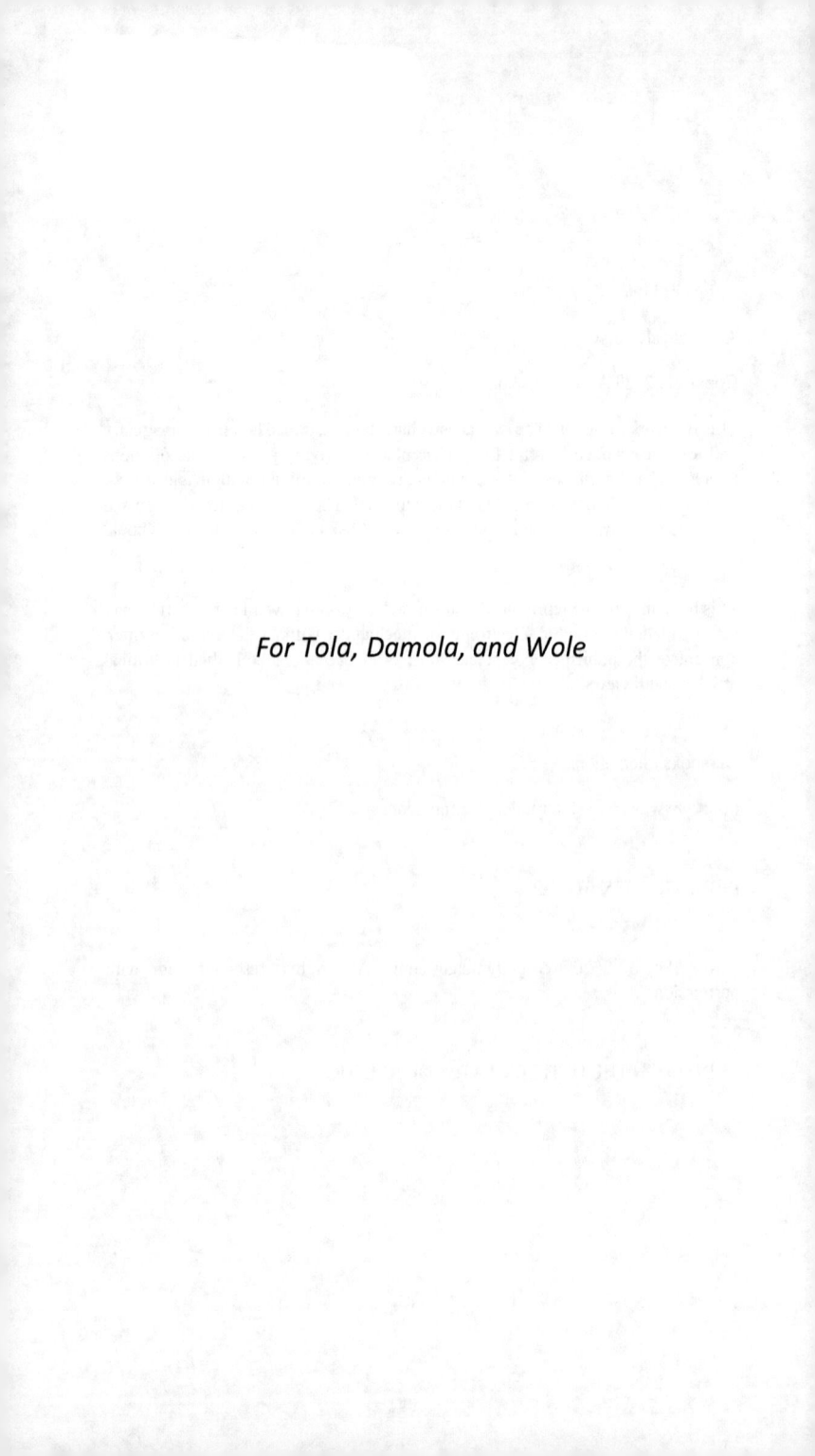

For Tola, Damola, and Wole

Colors
of
Love

ADEOLA OYEKOLA

Colors
OF
Love

Adeola Oyekola

PROLOGUE

In the shadow of love
Lies the secret of life.
My life I give to you
Never to take back.

In the shadow of love
Lies the lost truth.
Your life you give to me
Just for a while.

If love is true
Hate is a lie.
Then separate them
So that I can choose love.

Is this love?
Is this true?
Let us go deep down
To get the right meaning.

Life is too short
To be lived in agony.
Life is too short
To be lived in hatred.

Show me, Love.
Never deprive me of my innocence
Then run away.

If you do
My heart goes with you.
Leaving me empty
In a lonely world.

Stay with me.
Be truthful to me.
Stay with me.
Be gentle with me.

I am yours
Because you asked.
I am yours
Because you showed me love.

You have led me
To the sweetest side of life.
You have fed me
With delicious food for my heart.

So where shall I go
When you leave me?
So, what shall I eat
When you abandon me?

My heart thirsts for you.
My heart hungers for you.
You have planted your love
In my heart.

It has grown with a deep root.
It has flourished like a palm tree.
It has bloomed like the flower.
I can smell the fragrance.

How can I fill the vacuum?
How can I replace you?
How can I survive this?
How? How? How?

THE REUNION

CHAPTER 1

She sat on the porch, looking at the leaves falling from the trees. She remembered the lesson she watched her sister teach her kindergarten class about the different colors of leaves in the fall. Red, brown, yellow, and orange were falling, making a beautiful sight as the wind blew. The wind blew a red one onto her lap. She picked it up and looked at it for a long time, and she smiled. Her face gradually turned sad. It reminded her of her love life. A sad story. She scrunched it up in a fist and let the wind blow off the crumbs through her fingers.

Her mind flashed back to how it all started: in the woods, under the trees, the laughter, sweet emotions, warm kisses, and sweet embrace. It dawned on her that it wasn't all a sad story; there were moments of happiness also. She stood up and took a walk toward the small gate in her yard. She saw two boys riding bicycles on the street and laughing, oblivious of a moving vehicle. The car drove slowly behind them until there was enough space for it to drive off beside them. Thank God for patient drivers and intermittent humps. A woman yelled out from a house not too far away, telling them to get on the sidewalk. She was most likely their mother. They heeded the advice immediately as another car came driving by.

She took a walk down Chesapeake Street. After walking for about five minutes, she realized the need for a jacket. It wasn't as warm as she had thought. The fall weather was coming. "It was just as sunny as summer yesterday," she thought aloud. As she turned around, she heard someone call her. Before she could decide if it was real or not, she heard her name again, "Yeni!" "Yeni!" She turned around and saw Ralph running toward her. Speak of the devil! Too late to ignore him. She stood there and waited for him to join her.

"Hello Yeni," Ralph said, panting.

"Hello," Yeni replied.

"You were walking toward me, and I was patiently waiting, then you turned back."

"I wasn't walking toward you. I didn't see you at all."

"Well, I thought you did, and then you turned back," he said.

"Okay... achoo!" she sneezed before she could get the words out, and she did again and again!

"Bless you!" he said, concerned.

"Thank you," she replied between sneezes. "I was going back to get a jacket when you called me. Now, if you would excuse me, it's obvious I need one."

She walked away from him, back into her yard. Ralph watched her leave with his mouth slightly open. She decided not to go back outside, not after that encounter with Ralph.

Ralph lived on the next street to hers. She had met him on one of her numerous walks in the neighborhood. He had requested to join her in her walk that day. She let him, thinking that if she had company, it would help her to forget about her sad love story. She saw him as a needed distraction: he didn't see it that way, though. He wanted a girlfriend, the last thing she needed right now! He had tried to kiss her the other day, and she had slapped him right across the face; he was shocked and furious. She had not spoken to him since then, and that was two weeks ago. Yeni owed him an apology. He must have thought she was interested in him because she never said no to all his invitations to a walk. She lay on the couch and sneezed some more. She would never go outside without a jacket, not anymore!

On second thought, it might not be a jacket issue; it might be allergies! She had always associated sneezes with cold or the cold weather. Her sister made her understand that she must be allergic to something in the neighborhood, trees or plants of some kind. She had never heard about anyone being allergic to trees or flowers until her sister told her so. She thought about the different kinds of trees she'd played around with as a child, and about the various trees in her neighborhood back home. How come she never had allergies then? How come pollen never caused her eyes to be red and swollen in her home country? America is so different from Nigeria. "Allergic reaction, my foot! I need to go back home!" she exclaimed aloud.

She dozed off and woke to the sound of her phone ringing. She looked at the phone to see who the caller was, but it was an unknown number. She did not answer it. When the phone stopped ringing, she switched it off and went back to sleep. She needed the sleep before her nieces would come home from school. Only an hour away! She must have been sleeping for another ten minutes when the doorbell rang. "This is not my day..." she said as she dragged herself to the door. It was Carey, her best friend.

"Careyyyyy!" she screamed as she threw herself on her. They hugged and laughed and hugged some more.

"How did you find me?" Yeni asked.

"Well, don't I always find you?"

"Of course you do," Yeni said, between laughter, as her mind flashed back to their hide-and-seek games in middle school.

"Come on in," she said. "Good to have you around."

"My pleasure, girlfriend," said Carey.

"What do I offer you?" asked Yeni.

"Omoyeni Samson, always courteous. When will you change?" said Carey.

"Very good to hear you say my full name; haven't heard it said like that in a long time. So you stop the flattery, Carey. I should say the same thing about you."

"Oh, come off it, that's not flattery; it's the truth," Carey said, rolling her eyes.

"That's another thing you should stop doing, rolling those big eyes of yours." They both laughed.

"All right, girlfriend," Yeni said, "orange juice and Ritz crackers, okay?"

"Perfect," she said.

As Yeni walked away, her friend stared at her without blinking, and she said to herself, "She has seen better days."

Her heart sorrowed for her friend. Yeni was a gorgeous girl. Way back in Africa where their friendship began, she was the center of attraction for men. It didn't matter what hairstyle, or clothing style she had on, men would ask her out a couple of times before they noticed her friends. She was 5 feet, 6 inches with an average weight of 138 pounds which was about 62.5 kg. She was a tall slim light-skinned girl. She had long eyelashes, a long nose, black eyes, and her lips were just the right size for her face, not too big or too small.

Now, Carey thought, she surely must be only 100 pounds, if not less. She had lost so much weight that the laughter could not hide the sorrow in her eyes. Oh, how Carey's heart yearned for her! She had buried her sorrow in her heart for a long time. Hopefully, she would talk about it.

Yeni invited Carey into her room, where she had set out the refreshments. "We can stay here all day without disturbance. I hope you planned on sleeping over."

"Of course, I will. We have a lot to talk about."

The two friends were in an intense discussion when there was a knock on the door.

"Yeni, I'm back," said Tumi.

"Welcome, sis. You may come in; the door is not locked," answered Yeni.

The door opened to reveal an elegant lady whom Carey instantly knew was Yeni's sister; the resemblance was striking! They could have been identical twins, but for the difference in weight. Obviously, Yeni was slimmer than her older sister.

"You have a visitor?" Tumi asked, surprised.

"Yes, my best friend, Carey, all the way from..."

"Houston, Texas," Carey finished for her.

"Texas?" Yeni questioned.

Yes, I've been around for quite some time. Actually, about a year."

"Hmm, we'll talk about that later." Yeni turned to her sister.

"Like I was saying, meet my best friend, Carey, from Houston, Texas. We've been friends since our childhood. We attended the same schools and shared a lot of experiences. Carey, meet the sweetest sister in the world, Tumi."

"Nice to finally meet you, aunty," said Carey.

"Same here," replied Tumi. Yeni looked at both in wonder.

"Let me enlighten you, Yeni," said Carey. "I got Aunty Tumi's phone number from your mom in Nigeria but couldn't contact her until a few weeks ago when I found the piece of paper I wrote it on hidden in one of my purses. We both promised to keep my visit a secret from you until I arrive." She finished with a wink to Tumi.

"You both got me; I could never have thought..."

"I'll leave you girls to catch up on lost time," Tumi said. "The house is all yours; the kids are off for the night. They'll have a sleepover with their friends."

"Fantastic!" said Yeni. They all laughed as Tumi closed the door behind her. "The kids are terrible," Yeni informed Carey after her sister left.

"They'll be everywhere in minutes. You wouldn't believe they are all girls when you see the bursts of energy."

"Well, I still want to meet them," said Carey.

"You will, and they'll be back tomorrow. You said you'd been around for about a year in Texas?"

"Yes," Carey said.

"I came with my fiancé."

"Tell me something!" Yeni said excitedly.

"So," Carey began, "we met at a friend's party in Nigeria and we just clicked. He was on vacation from the US, and I was getting ready to come back to the US. He stayed a little longer for me to get my traveling papers together, and here we are," she finished, smiling.

"I am so happy for you, Carey," Yeni said, looking at her lovingly. "I'd like to meet with the man who could put such a sparkle in my friend's eyes."

"You'll meet very soon because you'll be visiting," Carey said with a big emphasis.

"Sure, I will," Yeni said excitedly. "I wish I had known you were close by; I would have been visiting."

"Now," Carey said, "it's your turn to talk, I want to know everything, I mean everything."

Yeni sighed, started to talk then stopped. Her countenance changed. Her eyes welled up with tears, and she tried to talk again. Then she burst into tears. Her friend held her in her arms and let her cry on her shoulder for a long time. Then she gave her a napkin to wipe her face and blow her nose. She offered her some water from the tray of refreshments set on the small table beside the bed. She refused the water but took the napkin, and shed a few more tears.

"I don't know where to start," she said after wiping her face.

"You can start from anywhere; flashbacks are acceptable." So, she began to tell her tale.

"I was in the lecture room that fateful day, at exactly 8:00 a.m. when the lecture was supposed to start. He was the only one in the class waiting for the lecture. I was surprised at the empty classroom, so I asked him, "Where is everybody?"

"I have no idea," was his response.

I pulled out my phone and gave you a call, and you told me the lecture was called off; you thought I received the message.

"Out of the whole class, only two of us didn't receive the cancellation notice?" he said with irritation. That was when I took a closer look at him. I had never met him before. It was our third year, and I was surprised that I wouldn't have known a course-mate of mine for three years. He introduced himself, and told me that he was carrying over the course as a minor course. That explained his strange face. I was mad at myself for waking up early to get to class. I could have slept for another hour or two. I mentioned this as we both exited the class and his response was, "There is a reason for everything." That was the beginning of my misery. We walked together for a long time, talking like old friends. We stopped by a restaurant and had breakfast together, and I found myself getting attracted to him."

THE STORY

CHAPTER 2

"Alan was a handsome young man. I don't have to describe him to you in great detail. Tall, light-skinned, well-shaped beard, curly hair—you name it -- everything attracted me to him. I had never been that close to a handsome man. They usually scared me until I met Alan. If I had only listened to you, if I had listened to my instincts, but I didn't. I was ready to enjoy the romance I believed was about to begin. We were friends for a while, and then we started dating. The day you met him, you told me he didn't seem like he would last. I disagreed with you.

Twelve months into our relationship, you gave up your doubts and accepted him as my boyfriend. He succeeded in fooling both of us. Then one day, I was in his room when his phone rang. He didn't answer it. Then it rang again, and I gave him the "What's going on?" look. So he answered it, and said to the caller that he was in class and he would call back later. I was shocked. "Alan, you're not in class. I need an explanation."

He said that was his cousin from his father's side, and he didn't want her to take away from our precious time together. I believed him. I was madly in love with him.

"We finished school, and we were all posted to different places for our National Youth Service Corp. I was in Enugu State; he was in Zamfara State. I was impressed when he redeployed to Enugu to be with me. Everyone believed in our blossoming love; even my parents had to accept him. We went on a surprise outing one day only to find out he was taking me to see his mom, who had just got back from the States. I should have known he redeployed not for my sake but because of her--since her residence was in Enugu State capital where I served. His mom was surprised to see me. I sensed a kind of coldness, but Alan said it was because she was meeting me for the first time.

He received that call again. This time, at the end of the call, he said, "Me too." That seemed suspicious to me. I asked him who the caller was. He said that was his cousin, again. He received the call again, another day. This time, he said he was with a friend.

'You can't tell her you are with your girlfriend?' I asked, getting a little jealous. He said no because she would go ahead and tell her dad who would think he was having a relationship that would keep him in Nigeria and he'd never go back to the States where he was needed to take over the leadership of his parents' company.

Then I asked him about what would become of our relationship after he left. He looked straight into my eyes, dipped his hand into his pocket, brought out a case, and opened it. There was a ring in it. He knelt on one knee and asked me to marry him. That was a great moment for me. Tears welled up in my eyes and rolled down my face just like right now. I asked him a question in response, I looked straight into his eyes and said, "You just said you were about to leave me for the States, how will it work if I marry you?"

He said some sweet words to me. I accepted his proposal. He promised to marry me before he would travel back to the States. Then he would process my visa, and I could join him. The plan was so exciting to me until I found out that I was pregnant.

All the time she was narrating her story, Yeni was standing by the window looking at the leaves falling from the trees. She turned around to face Carey, and she said "You wonder why a Christian should be pregnant outside marriage?"

Carey answered, "Yes."

"Uhm," Yeni continued, "I was a Christian, still a Christian. I was the Fellowship of Christian Students' (FCS) women's leader during my service year. Although I didn't plan on getting pregnant, I had sex with my boyfriend all the time. I did it because I wanted to, but I loved God. I still do. I guess I never let go when I fall in love, she said with a little laugh."

"But," Carey cut in, "how easy was it for you to be a Christian walking with God yet still sleeping with your boyfriend without a guilty conscience?"

"I had a guilty conscience, but I couldn't resist him, and I didn't feel like it affected my relationship with God. One thing I learned from it though is that, when he broke up with me, if I had not been that close to him, I would not have hurt as much as I did. That would also not have meant that I didn't give the whole of my love. I gave him more than he deserved. Some people do it, and I guess they end up marrying the same man because they are meant to be together, but in my case, I messed up my life. I am not over it yet.

"Introducing sex into a relationship is an extraordinary emotional commitment that is not easy for the female gender to get over quickly. If it results in pregnancy, it is worse. Pregnancy affects every aspect of a girl's life and only a little bit or none of a boy's. She gets to carry the baby, go through all the pains from the beginning, till the baby is born. Especially if the baby's arrival is sudden, the birth is bound to interrupt much in the mother's life. So, when God says something is wrong, it is not for His sake; it is for ours."

"I know that's right," Carey said. "It's my mom's saying that God has nothing to lose. The consequence, if you acknowledge his presence, is that you get encouraged."

Yeni sighed. "I was not thinking straight then. I was head over heels in love with Alan."

"What happened after you found out you became pregnant?" Carey asked.

"I told him I was pregnant," Yeni replied. "He said he was not ready for a baby. I said I wasn't either; it just happened. He didn't believe me. He said I got pregnant so that he would marry me. He called me different names: a gold digger, blackmailer, ungrateful, possessive -- you name it! He called me names I never knew existed."

"So, what did you do?" Carey asked, amazed.

"I was staring at him like I had seen a ghost," she replied. "We never fought. When arguments were getting heated up, he always slowed down and let me win the argument. It was always easy for him to apologize each time he thought he had offended me. That was why I was dazed as he ranted on and on until he said, 'You think you can ruin this for me right? I bet you can't!' And then he stormed out of my room. After he left, I broke down and cried like a baby. I didn't see him for the next two months. He didn't call, neither did I. I was not a gold digger. I was ready to face the consequence of what I did to myself; I was ready to be a single mother.

"Then he showed up with his mom on my last day in Enugu. I was still packing when they arrived. I was surprised to see them, but I offered them seats. They were silent for a long time. I guess the silence was becoming unbearable for them as it was for me, because I had to break the silence by asking them to what I owed the visit. His mom spoke for him. He had a wife. I guess the girl he told me about was his cousin. He only came to school in Nigeria because he wanted to meet his mother's side of the family and to learn the culture in Nigeria. He was more American than Nigerian. He had to return to the States to manage the family business—another reason why he studied Administrative Accounting.

"When she finished telling her story, I couldn't say a word. All I did was cry; I cried for wasted time, for believing lies, for allowing myself to fall a victim. The only question I asked them was about my pregnancy. I wanted to know what they would do about it. He had no answer. His mom wanted me to abort it. She also offered to give me enough money to start a new life, but I refused both offers. The meeting ended with another disturbing silence. I didn't sleep a wink that night. I traveled back to Lagos State with a heavy heart.

"That was another story entirely. What would I tell my family, especially my mom? The moment I stepped into the house, my mom knew something was wrong. I couldn't deny it. I spilled it all out, and she felt for me. She tried to talk me out of my sad mood to no avail. I carried the pregnancy for seven months and still had a premature stillbirth."

"What!" Carey exclaimed.

"It was devastating," Yeni continued. "My life has never been the same since. I had much pain during labor. Each time I remember the agony I went through, I shudder with pain and fright both mixed. I thought I was going insane. The more people sympathized with me, the more aggrieved I became. My life has been in a standstill ever since."

Carey stood up to give her friend a hug. They hugged and cried together. She felt her friend's pain. They calmed down about the same time and lay side-by-side on the bed. After a while, Carey asked,

"What happened after that?"

"My big sister, Tumi, sent me an invitation to come to the U.S. She thought a change of environment might be of help to me."

"Has it been helpful?"

"Yes and no. Yes, when I go shopping or sightseeing, and no when I am left alone to my thoughts, and no when I am left to babysit the kids. I remember my stillbirth baby whom I loved so much, to whom I diverted the love I'd had for her father."

"Did he call you to find out about you or the baby?" Carey asked.

"No, he didn't," she said with grief. "I wished he did and I would have excused his behavior to me, but he didn't. He did not love his child or me enough to ask after us. He has no faults; I am the fool. If I had listened to my pastor's sermon, or the church warnings about going through courtship without giving in to sex, my emotions would not have been so hurt. I feel like my life is damaged and irreparable. I condemn myself so much I feel like dirt."

"I have a question for you, Yeni. Do you still love him?"

"Did you just say, love?" Yeni replied, "I feel so much hatred for him that I wish I could kill him for what he did to me!"

"You need to free your mind. You need to let go of anger, hatred, and bitterness. Find a place in your heart to forgive yourself. I know you blame yourself so much, but you shouldn't. Listen, people fall in love like you did, get pregnant along the way, get married to the man they love, and they are Christians. Some, like you, get pregnant and become single parents and life continues for them. Others, like you, have lost both man and baby or pregnancy, and they move on with their lives. Some are Christians like you who have sex during their relationships, They either get married to the same man or not. Guess what? They move on with their lives. Nothing, I mean absolutely nothing, my friend, is worth dying for. You are walking around like a dead body and you are the shadow of yourself all because someone out there who did not deserve your love maltreated you. Life mistreats people but people fight back, and life gives them its goodness without a choice.

I have had my share of life's wickedness but, guess what, I move on. We'll talk about me some other day, not today."

"Carey, I am tired of my life. However, how do I go about creating a new life? I am not the same, I mean I don't know how."

"You have to start with prayer," Carey said. "Find a quiet time with God. Remember, you are not complaining to him; you are unburdening your heart to him. Ask for forgiveness, and the grace to move on with your life. You are stronger and wiser. Believe me, you are doing things differently, and with God on your side, you are standing tall again. America is the land of opportunities. You need to know what you want, and the result can be yours if you pursue it wholeheartedly."

Yeni got up and gave her friend a big hug. She thanked her and promised to heed her advice. She had never felt such relief in a long time. The two friends had a good time together for the three days Carey stayed there. Yeni promised to return the visit in a couple of weeks.

REVELATIONS

CHAPTER 3

arey woke up with a start. The air-conditioner was on, but she was sweating profusely. It was that dream again! What could it mean? In her dream, it was her wedding day, and there were numerous people waiting for the bride and groom to show up. She was ready for her day: a beautifully done hairstyle, and her face was perfect with makeup. She looked like the bride that she was in her long flowing white gown. Then she found herself asking, "Where is the groom?"

Could it mean something terrible was going to happen to her fiancé on their wedding day? Was it a scam? "A dream scam?" From who? Who knows, there are lots of scams out there these days. It might be the spirit world has some too!

"Come on, Carey," she said to herself, "you take things too lightly." This could be a severe preview. She knelt and said a simple prayer: "Lord, I thank you for this dream; it's been coming frequently. I don't know what to do about it. Please show me and lead me. For me, marriage is not a do or die affair, I sincerely love Tosin, and I believe he is my life partner. If there is something shady about him, reveal it to me before we begin wedding preparations. I want the best married life for myself. If it will not be successful, let me not get involved in it. However, if it will be helpful, I cancel every device of the enemy against it. In Jesus' name I pray. Amen."

She started getting ready for work. She went into the bathroom. As she showered, she sang William Murphy's worship song she loved so much: "Praise is What I do." She was so caught up in her worship that she lost track of time. She was running late! Her saving grace was that she had picked out her outfit the night before. She had chosen a black pantsuit with a red camisole -- a gift from Tosin. She matched it with black high heeled shoes and a black bag. She wore red lipstick with red eye shadow. Taking a quick look at herself in the mirror, she said, "Too hot for the devil. I am the wrong person to mess with." She grabbed her car keys and rushed out of her apartment. She was a secretary at a law firm. The Marcus family case was going to court that morning and she could not afford to be late. She said a brief prayer about the heavy traffic, scoffing a little afterward, thinking that was a waste of time. However, it was not. God favored her. An accident occurred right after the green light had allowed her to drive onto the main street.

It was a hectic day for her at work. When she checked her phone at work, she had missed six calls. Two of them were from her father. She hoped there was no problem. Two were from Tosin. He had left a heartwarming message for her. She smiled. One was from Yeni, and the last one was unknown. There were three calls to return.

She decided to call Tosin first, then her dad. Tosin just wanted to hear her voice. His words took some work tension off her. She promised to call him back on her way home. Then she called her dad. He wanted to know if she liked her new job and new apartment. She said she did and that was it. Then she called Yeni back. She was happy to hear that she was terrific and that she had found her interest in hairdressing. Her sister's friend, Ihuoma, who owned a hair salon, was allowing her to come in to help. She was in a sort of apprenticeship, and she got a few dollars every week. Another exciting thing that happening to Yeni was that she had joined a Bible-believing church. Her mind was busy and she was moving on with her life. Carey was happy for her. She needed to give her mom a call. It had been about three days since their last discussion She would call her when she got off. As she rose from lunch, she received a text message from Tosin. "Dinner tonight?"

"Sure. What time?"

"Seven?"

"Where?"

"Dino's Steak. I'll pick you up."

"Seven-thirty."

"See you then!"

"Loverboy," she said under her breath, smiling.

It was 3:30 p.m. She was winding things up for the day, and was thinking about her date tonight. She got off at 4:00; she had thirty minutes to drive home, maybe forty-five, with traffic. She would barely get some rest before the date. Selecting the right outfit might take her some time. Tosin was very romantic, and he liked sexy outfits. At a quarter to 4:00, a package was delivered to her. It had her name boldly written on it. Who could it be from? She waited until she got into her car before she opened it, it was a lovely red dress sent by Tosin. He was too romantic. She called him, told him she loved the dress but loved him more.

"See you tonight…"

Carey woke up with a headache. It was unseasonably warm the night before she had the air on again. She must be coming down with something, hopefully not the flu. As she rolled over in bed, her mind went back to the night before. During the dinner, did she see a shadow under Tosin's eyes when she said they should fast and pray? Surely he wasn't hiding anything from her.

The food was good, and the wine tasted even better. Carey was enjoying the evening, giggling from ear to ear at Tosin's frequent jokes. She was feeling very relaxed in his company, as usual. Then he became quiet and was staring at her lovingly. She felt naked as he seemed to undress her with his stare.

"What?" she asked.

"I want to marry you," he said softly, "I want you waking up in my bed every day. I want to see you carrying my babies and making my home a comfortable place for me. Carey, I want our wedding preparations to commence immediately."

Silence. Carey felt her heart beating so loudly that she thought he could hear it.

"Carey, say something."

"The d-d-dream," she stammered.

"What dream?"

"The dream I told you about the last time, I had it again last night," she blurted it out.

Sitting back with a sigh and folding his arms, Tosin said,

"What about it?"

"I think we should pray," she said.

"About what? I already told you that I am not about to die, and I am not running away on our wedding day. I love you too much to do that to you. You are getting unnecessarily anxious."

"Okay, how about we go to church for pre-marital counseling?" she suggested.

"I don't get it, Carey. The dream is about me, and I'm not worried, why are you?"

"Because I love you, and you will soon be a part of my life. It's not like I'm worried, I just think I'm having these dreams so that we can do something about it."

"I am not going to counseling with you."

"But why not?"

"Your father is part of the team. What do you think he would say? He'll probably discourage you from marrying me."

"Okay, Tosin, will you do me a favor? Let's have a two-day fasting and prayer and ask God to reveal the plan of the enemy concerning our wedding. After the prayer period, we can then go ahead and let our parents know that we want to begin wedding plans. Is that too much to ask?"

"No, it's not," he said sadly.

As she lay on her bed, ruminating over the event of the past evening, she could only pray that nothing would come between her relationship with him. When she eventually got out of bed, she had to hurriedly get ready for work. She was running late.

That day was uneventful. She bought dinner on her way home. She sat in front of the TV, watching her favorite show as she ate. It was past 11:00 p.m. when she finally fell asleep on the couch. She woke up to her phone ringing; it was her mom. Carey had told her several times to add five hours to Nigerian time before making a call. Carey was lucky the phone stopped ringing before she could answer. Her mother would call her back in the morning. She really needed the sleep. The following day was the beginning of her fasting and prayer, and she was not going to add a sleepy head to that.

She woke up with her alarm and phone ringing at the same time. With one hand, she turned the alarm off; with the other, she answered her phone.

"Hello…" she said sleepily.

"Hello, my dear…"

"Good morning, Mom…"

"Good morning, were you still sleeping…?"

"Yes, but it's okay. It's time to wake up."

"Can you call me back?"

"Okay, give me a few minutes…"

She hung up and worried about what her mother was going to say to her. It must be something important for her to call late last night and early this morning. She went into the bathroom, took a shower and brushed her teeth. Then she called her mom back and put the phone on speaker while she dressed. That usually saved her some time, especially with calls that lasted a long time like her mother's and especially when she was getting ready for work. After the usual pleasantries, her mom told her what her friend had said about Carey.

"I had a prayer date with my friend, Eniola," her mother told her. "After the prayers, a word of knowledge came through her for you. The Lord wanted you to be careful about decision making, especially when it comes to the choice of a life partner."

"Did you say a prayer date? What does that mean?" Carey responded.

"It means I chose a day to pray with my friend and prayer partner, we both fasted and prayed about the burdens on our hearts..."

"I have always told you not to talk about me with your prophets and pastors," said Carey. They always have something to say that I don't want to hear."

Her mom swallowed the anger that was about to burst through her before she said, "I did not go to a prophet or a pastor. I had a prayer date with my friend, and I did not go there to pray for you. I went to pray for my family, and you are one of them. I want you to pray very hard before you choose a life partner. I know you told me you were thinking about getting married but be sure that you're making the right decision. Have a great day at work." She hung up.

Carey called her mom back and apologized to her about her response to the revelation. She confided in her that she was starting a two-day fasting and prayer over the issue. While driving to work, Carey thought about her dream and her mom's words and shuddered. She loved Tosin too much to give him up now. Were her mom's words the answer to her prayers? No, that couldn't be' She did not say she shouldn't marry him; all she said was to be careful. However, "careful" is loaded with meaning. She needed to unravel the mystery.

"Lord, please, show me a sign. Unravel this mystery. I am about to burst with anxiety!"

Gracefully for her, it was a busy day at work so she had no time for personal worries. She called her friend, Yeni, on her lunch break. They had lots to chat about; the most exciting part was that Yeni would be visiting that weekend. She couldn't wait.

When the weekend came, they did everything together. The two friends cooked, shopped and went to eateries. They were shopping at Macy's on Sunday evening when Susan walked up to them. She stood in their way and stared at Carey for a long time.

"Excuse me," Carey said. Susan changed her look to a mean one.

"I said, excuse me," she repeated.

"I heard you the first time," Susan said, "but I won't budge. Well, you look beautiful. I can see why he chose you over me, but I will not be used and dumped. That's why I want you to know that if you eventually get married to Tosin, you will be legally married to him but I will be his chosen love partner. I wouldn't mind sharing him with you 'cos you are beautiful... If you know what is good for you, you will stay away from him. He's not a one-woman man."

She left the girls speechless.

"Who was that?" Yeni asked.

"I have no idea," Carey said. Just then, Susan walked back to them.

"I am sorry I didn't introduce myself. I am Susan, Tosin's lifetime girlfriend." Carey gasped. "Don't be shocked," Susan continued. "It's a game; you will get used to it in a short while." Then Susan walked away, her chin in the clouds.

THE BROKEN HEART

CHAPTER 4

The silence in the car on the drive home was uncomfortable. Carey had run out of the store into the safety of her car. Yeni ran after her, yelling out her name. Yeni had expected her to burst into tears, but she did not. She sat there for a long time, looking straight ahead but in deep thought. Yeni talked to her, but she refused to reply. After a while, Carey began the drive home.

The silence was very uncomfortable. Yeni didn't know what to do. Then, on impulse, she turned on the radio. Kirk Franklin's song "My Life is in Your Hands" was on. Carey motioned to turn the radio off, but she stopped as her fingers touched the tuner. Tears rolled from her eyes. Yeni looked at her with empathy and asked if she would let her drive.

Carey shook her head. "I got it," she said. Yeni was relieved that she, at least, said something. When they got back to Carey's apartment, she went straight to her room and picked up Tosin's picture from her dresser. She said, "Tosin, why would you do this to me?" The sobs came softly and grew louder.

Yeni held her close in an embrace and cried with her friend. She knew the pains of heartbreak. She could feel for her friend.

Why would men be ruthless all in the name of love? However, was this even love? Is deceit love?

"Love is patient, and love is kind. It does not envy, and it does not boast. It is not proud. It does not dishonor others, and it is not self-seeking. It is not easily angered. It keeps no record of wrongs." She'd recited this passage in her head as many times as possible. She remembered it each time a man tried to get close to her. How could men be so cruel and heartless? Showing a woman so much love and making her fall in love with them and then breaking her heart? She thought it was the height of evil. Carey calmed down and released herself from her friend's embrace, sat on her bed, took her shoes off, and lay on the bed. She was in deep thought. Yeni did the same beside her. They were in this same position when Yeni told her the story of her love life with Alan. Yeni broke the silence, "A penny for your thoughts, please."

"Could it be true? Yeni, could it? I mean, how can I explain the fact that Tosin is hiding such a secret from me? Moreover, he is cheating on me, too?" She was now getting angry

"I am glad you're talking," Yeni said, "The only way we can find out the truth is if you confront him with what you know. Who knows? Susan could be a jealous ex-girlfriend."

"Why wouldn't he tell me about her if she was his ex? I want to believe that this is the answer to the mysterious dreams I've been having. I knew something was fishy."

She received a text message, picked up her phone and whispered, "Speak of the devil." With that, she threw her phone. Fortunately, it missed the wall. It landed on the pile of clothes in her closet. Yeni got up, picked up the phone, and read the message:

"Hey, love! Just missing you."

"Why not give him a call?" Yeni said, giving her the phone.

"I don't want to talk to him!" Carey said.

"In fairness to him, you owe it to him to hear him out," Yeni continued. "How about you invite him over and ask him about Susan? You don't know Susan. She could be a blackmailer for all you know." In response, Carey took the phone and texted him back: "Do you mean you miss Susan? When were you going to tell me about her? Well, she can have you to herself; you don't need me."

Tosin read the text message and almost had a heart attack.

He dialed Susan's office number. He heard her voice from the other end, "Good afternoon, GG Associates. How may I help you?"

"You may help me by fixing the damage you have done!" He lashed out. "How could you? You talked to her after I told you not to. You are ridiculous!"

Tosin was fuming with anger.

"Slow down, lover boy. I'm at work," Susan replied slowly." How about we talk later?"

"We talk right now!"

"You must excuse me; I have another call on line two." She put him on hold to receive other calls. Each time he called, she hung up on him. She finally excused herself to go home, blaming it on a family emergency. Upon leaving the building, she was face to face with Tosin.

"You scared me!" she said, after bumping into him.

"I will do more than scare you if you don't make right what you did wrong," Tosin growled.

"You are not trying to make a scene at my work, are you?"

She walked away, and he followed her. They went to their usual spot, and spoke at length. Susan made him realize that he could not just walk away from her after five years of an intimate relationship. She had had a series of abortions, and he had promised to marry her. She said she would only allow him to marry another girl if he could make her pregnant again before he walked away. Susan said she was over with men because of the way he treated her and was ready to be a single mom. Tosin thought he had no choice but to agree. However, she wanted to be pregnant before she would go back to Carey and make her believe that she had blackmailed him.

Meanwhile, after she went home alone, Carey was in deep thought. She couldn't sleep. Her mom called and sensed something was wrong with her daughter, but Carey waved aside her fears. She couldn't tell her. How could she? When she was hoping all would still be well between them.

"Oh, God, let this all be a very bad dream!" she said and burst out crying. Yeni heard Carey crying. She rushed out of the room to the living room. Yeni stood still for a little bit watching her crying. She then walked up to her and held her in a tight hug.

"Has he replied to your text message?"

She shook her head as fresh tears began to roll down her cheeks.

"I guess there is no explanation," she said between sobs. "I don't know what to do."

"It's too early to make any decisions," Yeni said. You need to relax. "I believe he has some explanations for what Susan told us. Just then, his text message came in. "I don't know what Susan told you, but it must be a lie. She is a blackmailer. We need to talk about this right now. Can I come over?"

Carey replied, "Yes." He was hoping to spend the night at Carey's. As Yeni popped her head out of the bedroom to offer a greeting, his heart sank. He had thought of sweet-talking Carey to bed after a brief conversation. It wasn't going to work out that way with her friend in the apartment.

"Have you come here to stare at my friend or to talk?" Carey asked irritated.

"I'm sorry," Tosin said, "I was hoping you would introduce your visitor."

"That's not why you are here..."

"Omoyeni--Yeni works better," she said, offering him a handshake.

"Tosin," nice meeting you," he said, shaking her hand.

"I hope I can say that too," Yeni said, sending him a dagger with her eyes.

"I'll leave you two alone to sort things out." She went back into the other room.

"I am all ears, Tosin," Carey said, sitting down, "you may take a seat."

"What did she tell you?" Tosin asked.

"Who is 'she'?" Carey said.

"I mean Susan. What did she tell you?"

"Why would you want to know? I want to hear it from you."

He sighed. None of his planned tricks seemed to be working. He had thought he could use Carey's words against her but now, she was not talking.

"If you have nothing to say, you may leave. I believe Susan told me everything I needed to know," Carey said, close to tears.

"No, no, I do have something to say. Susan is my ex. She wants our relationship to continue, but I have always refused every one of her attempts to come back to me. I love you, not her, and she knows this.

Therefore, she came to you to try to ruin our relationship."

"Your ex? Why didn't you ever say anything about her? Your ex who dared to walk up to me and tell me that she was your lifetime girlfriend — that she wouldn't mind sharing you with me? Are you a piece of meat? She is okay with sharing, but I am not. You have not been able to convince me that she is your ex. Please leave me alone. I need to be alone."

"You have to believe me, Carey. We are no longer together," Tosin pleaded.

"I said, get out! Carey said and burst into tears. He tried touching her, and she screamed. Yeni came out of the room, opened the door for him, and gave him the same cold stare. He left. After his departure, Yeni allowed her friend to cry a little longer, and then she asked her, "What do you think?"

"I think he's telling a lie," she replied, brokenhearted.

"I think so, too," her friend agreed. "I couldn't help hearing everything that he said. So, what's next?"

"What if he loves me and he wants to stop the relationship with Susan? Maybe we can still work things out... Maybe if he..."

"Maybe what, Carey? What he is doing is called double dating. If he can double date at this stage in your relationship, then he would at one point or more in your married life have a secret affair. Moreover, just like it happened, you would pray and God would reveal the secret to you, and it would be harder for you to handle then than now. I am your friend; I will not hide my feelings from you. I say quit. It might not be easy for you to do it, but I say quit. I am going to bed; I want you to join me very soon. Goodnight."

Neither Yeni nor Carey could sleep that night. Yeni was thinking about her experience with Alan and couldn't help linking it with that of her best friend. Why did they have the same things in common? Well, maybe not everything because Carey was not pregnant. Yeni knew her friend loved Tosin so much, and it wasn't going to be easy for her to break up with him. She also knew that Tosin would come back with more lies and it was possible that her friend would fall back into his trap.

Moreover, Carey was not sharing with her mom -- sharing the situation with her would have made it easier for her to break up with him. Yeni loved her friend so much and did not want her to go through any more emotional trauma. However, she could do nothing to stop this. It was her friend's decision.

Then she thought about why she had not given any other man a chance. She knew she was afraid of another heartbreak. Looking at her friend hurting was a good reason for her to keep on running away from men, but that night, another thought crept into her heart. If she was able to detect that Tosin was telling a lie, it would mean that her experience with Alan was worth it. She also thought that if God could answer Carey's prayer by exposing her fiancée's secret, then she could trust God to do the same for her. Carey's story seemed a fantastic testimony to her. She only prayed that her friend would take heed and flee for dear life instead of thinking that he would change.

Then her thoughts switched to that of the men that had been asking her out. She thought about Peter who worked in the same school where her sister was a kindergarten teacher. She smiled when she remembered the way he handed her a flower with the silly uneasy look on his face. She thought of how clumsy he was when he was talking to her. He was a wimp. She couldn't have fallen for him. Then she thought about Edward. Edward was a replica of Alan. That kind of irritated her. She didn't need another Alan, not in this world or the next one. Then she thought about Ralph, her neighbor. Interestingly, a warm feeling crept up in her heart for him. She had been too hard on him, she admitted, and she kept on postponing the apology.

She gave him a dirty slap! That was uncalled for. She could have, maybe, pushed him away or taken a step backward. He had tried several times after the incident to talk to her. Perhaps she could give him a chance. Maybe, just maybe…

Carey, on the other hand, was thinking about how she could fix her already broken relationship. She wouldn't tell her parents. Carey would wait for him to call her again and give him audience. She would make him promise to cut off the relationship with Susan, ask God for forgiveness, and they could go ahead and get married. If prayers could reveal the secret, prayers should fix a repentant heart. She would marry him, and they would live happily ever after. However, what if he loved Susan more than he loved her? What if Susan lived up to her threat and kept him as her secret lover? What if what Yeni said came true? What if he became unfaithful in their marriage?

Tears rolled down her face again. She had to call her mom. She needed motherly advice. She cried herself to sleep. When her alarm clock rang in the morning, she called in sick.

Yeni left early the next morning with a promise to give her a call every day. She left only after a prayer with her.

A MOTHER'S EXPERIENCE

Omolara Jackson did not hesitate to board the next available flight to the U.S. after she heard what her daughter had to say about her fiancé. Out of her four children, Carey was the one she worried most about, all because she lived far away from her. Carey had always been a "daddy's girl." Omolara did not like the idea of her daughter living by herself, but she had no choice. A 28-year-old girl is old enough to live her life the way she wants it. She only prayed that her daughter would listen to the voice of reason and let Tosin go. From what she'd heard of him, she concluded he was a cheat and not fit for her daughter.

Fourteen hours on the airplane was not a joke. She would have enjoyed it like she always did if not for the fact that she was worried about her daughter. She didn't want her to make the same mistakes she made that landed her where she was — an older single woman. She smiled at the category she grouped herself into — single woman, not mother — because none of her children lived with her. At 58, she looked like she was in her mid-forties. What a loss for James Jones, who deserted her when she needed him the most!

It was a pity that her arrogant lifestyle landed her in trouble. She lived in regret and didn't wish that any of her children should be in her shoes. She had three girls and a boy. Carey was the last of them. She wished

Carey had listened to her and stayed back in Nigeria with her. How sad that she had no control over the decision!

Her mind went back to how she met James Jones. She was very young and fresh out of college. She was just twenty-two and was ready to get her first job. She was one of the lucky young scholars who, because they were brilliant, got admitted into the universities early. She was beautiful, knowledgeable, arrogant and she made straight A's.

Her life soared in bright colors. She only dated boys from luxurious homes and never talked to boys who were struggling to survive. That was how she met James. She had visited her friend, Rashida, in Lagos Island when she met him. He was a visitor from the USA and was going to stay with Rashida's family for about three months. He liked her, and she loved him too. When he asked her out, she was prudent enough to ask Rashida about him. She told her he was her daddy's business partner, but she said he had a family in America.

Omolara was sad at the realization that he was married, and he was asking her out. She confronted him with the story, but he was shrewd enough to let her know that he was married to a white lady, but he wanted to add a Nigerian wife. According to him, he was in the middle of a divorce with his white wife. If everything worked out well between him and

Omolara, he would marry her. Things went well until she got pregnant before anybody could assess their relationship as either working out or not. Her father disowned her. He was disappointed in her because he was already thinking of talking to her about getting a master's degree since she was still young.

James did not disappoint her; he got her an expensive apartment and lavishly furnished it. She lacked nothing, at least nothing money could buy. However, he never married her. She was his mistress for nine years. Her father would not give her hand to him in marriage. Within nine years she had three children. She found out on their tenth anniversary that he did not marry her because he was still married to the white lady and not because her father was adamant. She cried herself sore. She lamented that he had cheated her. However, he denied the allegation.

Omolara was invited to Houston, Texas, by one of her friends, and she traced James to his home. She saw his wife and his two children and introduced herself as his wife from Nigeria. He denied her. She aimed to let the cat out the bag so that his wife would divorce him, and he would have no choice but to marry her, but that didn't work. He said he would rather stay single or marry another woman from the States if his white wife should divorce him. According to him, Omolara was kind enough to care for his children. She was his Nigerian mistress. She'd better stay that way, or she would never see him again.

She was devastated. If he treated her that way, then she could do it too. One night, she went to the club with her American friend, got drunk, and woke up in a strange bed. It was Jackson's bed. He had liked her since the first day he set his eyes on her. He didn't touch her in the wrong way. He helped her home because she was drunk. She eventually had an affair with him which resulted in Carey.

Like her previous relationship, he wouldn't marry her. He was engaged but had lied to her. Omolara had had her fair share of regrets in life, and she didn't want Carey to go in the same direction. If this Tosin boy was a cheat, she wanted him out of her daughter's life at all cost. She was ready to share her life story with her daughter.

Carey, on the other hand, oblivious of her mother's journey, was happy to have a busy day. She was neck-deep in sorting out files and rearranging her new office. Carey needed the heavy load of work to keep her mind away from her relationship. It was heading for the rocks, or was it already on the rocks? She shivered each time she thought about it. The bitter truth was that she was not ready to let it go. She loved him so much. She had returned his text message the night before. She wanted him to give her some time to think the whole situation through. She pushed the thought out of her mind as she worked. She quickly grabbed an offer to work late. Yeni had returned to Washington, DC so, Carey was going to return to an empty house. She would rather stay at work than return to empty silence.

She was surprised when she saw her mother walk through the doorway into her office. She rushed to her to give her a warm embrace. Tears of joy rolled down her cheeks, and she repeated, "I love you, Mom. You couldn't have come at a better time." She gave her mom the keys to her apartment and put her on a cab. "Go home and wait for me. I must work late today because I accepted the work. I should be with you in about three hours. Call me as soon as you get into the apartment.

Omolara settled inand she was glad to have a warm apartment to herself. She made herself a cup of coffee with some biscuits she found in the refrigerator. She had dozed off when Carey walked in. She was so tired she didn't even stir in her sleep when Carey walked in. Carey cleared the coffee table of her empty cup of coffee and paper napkin of biscuits. She undressed and was walking past her sleeping mom on the couch into the kitchen when she woke up.

"Oh, you're back," Omolara said, in between a yawn.

"Yes Mom, I didn't want to wake you. I knew you were exhausted from the long journey."

Omolara agreed that she was fatigued and when she said she thought it was old age, they both agreed that was true. But Carey insisted that she didn't look her age. Carey suggested to her mom to get a hot bath while she made dinner.

While her mother was in the bathroom, Carey opened a can of beef soup, dumped it into a pot and let it simmer for a couple of minutes. She then added some powdered hot pepper to give it that spicy taste her mother loved. While waiting on the soup, Carey toasted some slices of bread and made tuna. She also had available her favorite kale salad. The table was ready by the time her mother came out of the bathroom. She knew her mother would eat the salad first.

Dinner went smoothly. They talked about things in general: her job, her siblings, her dad, and they were both yawning at 11:00 p.m.

When Omolara suggested that they should go to sleep so she wouldn't be late for work the next day, she said she would have taken the day off, but there was a lot to be done at work. She would finish setting up her office the next day, which was a Tuesday and find out if she could get a colleague to work for her on Wednesday. That way, she could spend a whole day with her mom. Her mother wanted her to go to work every day because she would have the entire weekend with her. Besides, she would be waiting for her after work every day.

They spoke about almost everything but never mentioned that night the reason why she came. However, they got to it the next day. Her mom had prepared her local delicacy before she returned from work. It was her favorite greens soup cooked with three different blends of pepper: bell pepper, habanero pepper, dry chili red peppers and onions, popularly called "efo riro." She added three different kinds of seafood: dried shrimp, dried catfish, and stockfish. She also made some "poundo yam". Carey didn't take her work outfit off before she went for the food. She was appreciative as she ate. The spicy taste was the best part of the meal. Omolara offered to do the dishes while Carey took a bath.

They were both seated in front of the TV when Omolara broached the subject of her visit. She wanted to hear everything that transpired between Carey and Tosin. Carey told her story without leaving anything out. Omolara said almost the same thing that Yeni said — she wouldn't lie to her. She said outright that Tosin was a cheat. He might claim to love her, but she didn't believe in such a love that keeps secrets and other affairs. What would he do after they were married? Then she went ahead to narrate the story of her life.

"I want you to learn from my mistakes and not repeat them. The decision is yours to make, but I want you to be reasonable." She further explained to her that all her other siblings were happily married and she would want Carey to be too. She didn't want any of her children to suffer from the hands of a man like she had. Love in the right direction is the best thing that could happen to a woman. Carey promised to think about it because she still hadn't made up her mind to let go. She'd asked him to give her two weeks to "think" about the situation.

Her mother prayed with her on the issue that night before they went to sleep. She knew she couldn't do more than pray and advise her. The decision was for her to make. Carey couldn't sleep for a long time after the discussion with her mom. She knew she wanted her to break up with Tosin but she couldn't. Breaking up with him didn't sound right. What would she tell her friends and colleagues? Most of her church members knew she was getting close to getting married. What would she tell them? She was already thinking of settling down and getting pregnant, having babies, and living a happy married life. What would happen to that? Should she just let Susan take away what belonged to her?

"If Tosin is choosing me over her, then I am the winner." That was her thought.

"I shouldn't let the devil possess my possession. Tosin keeps saying he loves me, not Susan. That's all I need. I mean I should be proud of the fact that out of two women, I am the chosen one. I think my prayer point should be for God to make everything possible for me to marry Tosin. He needs my prayers to stay faithful to me, and he needs my prayers for our love to stand. I think I will start praying right away." She did. Her prayer points were for God to keep Tosin for her, give him the grace to stay away from other women and for him to love her more. With that prayer said, she fell asleep. What she didn't know was that while she was praying, Tosin was spending the night with Susan. He needed to get her pregnant.

THE DECISION

CHAPTER 6

Yeni came visiting again. She wanted to see Omolara before she went back to Nigeria. It was another excellent time for Carey. Having her mother and her best friend with her for that weekend was a great joy. What a blessing to have such loving people around her! She had requested that her mother would visit her dad with her, but she refused.

"If he wanted to see me, he would come looking for me. I didn't come here to see him; I came to see you."

"Come on, Mom, it's just a visit," Carey pestered.

"Can we talk about something else? This topic is boring," Omolara said.

They went to the hair salon instead. After shopping, they went back home to watch a movie on LMN. Omolara was asleep before the movie was over. Carey surmised that had it been a Nigerian movie, she wouldn't have fallen asleep in the middle of it. They had watched a series of Nigerian movies together the weekend before. This weekend with Yeni was awesome. They had a lot to talk about.

Yeni had requested to move out of Tumi's home, and she had reasoned with her. Yeni told them about her new job as a hairdresser. She loved it. She would have loved to continue as a teacher like she was in Nigeria, but because her status in America was still that of a visitor, she couldn't. The Nigerian lady who happened to be her sister's friend had enrolled her as one of her apprentices. She learned very fast and graduated as a professional hairstylist. It was also easy for her to braid hair, an art she had perfected in her high school years. Fixing people's hair was easy for her; she seemed to have the perfect touch for every hairstyle. She only worked whenever she wanted to. What she was making was enough for her to pay bills and fend for herself. She was able to rent a room in a three-bedroom apartment. One of her sister's colleagues rented a three-bedroom apartment, but she only used one of the rooms. She sub-let the other two rooms. That way, she was able to keep up with the bills.

Yeni usually worked very hard the first two weeks in the month to make enough money for the booth she rented, her apartment rent and utilities. She regularly worked four days a week for the next two weeks. She enjoyed her independent life. She had nobody to boss her around. She knew how to do different kinds of braids and hairstyles. She had enough customers to be thankful for. She was usually booked out for the month by the first of every month, and her clients showed up regularly. If one didn't, she took walk-ins, or called in "bystanders." Whenever she had a booked-up schedule for the month, she put some clients on the standby list, and she called them whenever she had a canceled appointment, which rarely happened.

"It's good to be good at what you do," Carey said, as Yeni finished telling her about her job.

"You can say that again," Yeni replied. Her only regret was her immigration status. She had thought about going back to Nigeria before her visa expired but didn't find it realistic. The experience she had there was too much for her. She had nothing to go back to but an empty lifestyle and old painful experiences. She filed for an extension of stay. Another six months was approved. Hopefully, she would be able to change her immigration status before her two-year visa would lapse.

It was Carey's turn to say something, and she was hesitating. So Yeni asked her what development there was in her relationship with Tosin. Her mom and her friend waited patiently for an answer.

She told them she had made up her mind to forgive him and go on with the wedding as they had both planned. She said to them that she had a heart-to-heart discussion with him and he confessed to her that he was dating her and Susan at the same time because Susan wouldn't let go of him. He told her that he loved Carey and would do anything to have her as his wife. He also told her he had broken up with Susan and would never hook up with her again. That was a promise. She said she thought about it and decided to forgive him since he had told her the truth and he had repented. Everyone abhors sins sometimes. "Besides,

I still love him; he's my dream man. You need to see him pleading with me on his knees and shedding tears like a baby. That's my decision. What do you think?" she expressed more of a conclusion than a question.

Omolara and Yeni exchanged looks. They were both silent for a long time. When the silence became unbearable, Carey walked to the window. She was staring at the empty winter street, feeling as cold as the weather on the inside. Her loved ones' silence could only mean disapproval. What would she do if she lost the love and friendship of her mother and best friend? Would Tosin's love for her be able to fill in for theirs? Yeni walked up to her and put her hands around her. "Is that your final decision?" She asked.

Carey whispered, "Yes."

"I know I would have loved to hear you say you were breaking up with him, but since you chose to go ahead with him, I have no choice but to respect your decision." Carey was grateful. She gave her a big hug and said a big thank you. She walked over to her mother and asked her what she thought again. Her words were few.

"You want to marry him after I have shared my life story with you? My story didn't mean anything to you?"

"Mom, the men in your life didn't want you. They chose other women over you but my man has chosen me over the other woman. I wouldn't let the other woman take my man away from me," Carey concluded.

"I guess it's a competition," was Omolara's response. "Well," her mother said, "you have three examples to learn from: my story, Yeni's story, and your dreams. If after considering all of these, you still choose to marry him, then so be it. However, it would be my joy for you to break up this relationship."

"I believe that's a yes!" Carey said. She hugged her mom as tears rolled from her eyes. It was coming true; she was getting married to her tall, handsome dark-skinned guy. They would make an excellent family together.

That night, Omolara couldn't sleep. She thought of finding out who the Susan girl was. That would not be at all easy. If it were in Nigeria, she would know some people who could do the job for her, but in Houston, Texas, she knew nobody. She thought of praying some more. Maybe God would change her daughter's mind from getting married to him, but God is not a magician. He breaks the human heart in His own time. How could this be happening to her daughter? She prayed wholeheartedly for her daughter's future. She then left it all in God's hands and went to sleep. She had a dream, but when she woke up, she couldn't remember the dream. However, she felt a soothing calmness within her. She knew God was in control.

That was why she had the right answer for Carey the next morning.

Carey came to her room to bid her good morning. She also added that her mom shouldn't worry about her because she was old enough to know what was right for her. Omolara responded by saying: "You are right. You are old enough to choose what is right for you. That is why God gave you the repeated revelations, my story, and Yeni's story. You know the truth about Tosin; God is allowing you to make a choice. I want you to know that marrying him is your choice, not mine, and not God's. Just remember that when you need God, He will be waiting for you. I am a human being. I cannot be there as much as God would, but I will do everything within my power to give you the support you need any time. I love you and always will."

"I know you love me, Mom. That's why you came down here when you heard how broken-hearted I sounded on the phone. I will not let you down, I promise."

"My fear is not your letting me down; my fear is you letting God down. Whatever happens, you should know that you can always run to God in sincerity of heart. He will not despise you." She prayed with her and asked to see Tosin before she would leave the next day.

As for Yeni, she had little or nothing to say. "Your decision is my decision. You want it, and I am with you in it." She hugged her friend goodbye early the next morning, making her promise she would be the first to know whenever there was a date set for the wedding.

On her way back to Washington, DC, Yeni was in deep thought. She was encouraged by the boldness with which Carey made her decision. Yeni thought she had made the wrong decision, no doubt about that. But she was bold about it, and she knew she would be ready for any challenge that might face her in the future. She asked herself several times why she chickened out of situations, froze at every problem, or refused to move on with her life whenever she faced a dead end.

She thought about Ralph. She could mend fences with him and give him a chance. She would be cautious and use a different approach this time. She would use the church principles this time. She hoped it would work out. She was not ready to take the risk of giving in all her wifely duties before her marriage and then end up broken without a wedding. Once beaten, twice shy. Never would it happen again!

She had also thought that Tumi, her older sister, was blessed and favored. She had everything: money, beauty, children, good job, great husband, elegant lifestyle. What more could she think of? Some people still get it together in life despite ups and downs. She was sometimes jealous of her sister's family life. She should ask her a few questions someday. Why should she live with such a great lady and not have secrets of a successful family life? She had witnessed a couple of arguments between the couple but the next minute they were back together chatting and laughing. She thought that was awesome.

There was an occasion when her sister was angry at her husband. She left the house for about four hours after the argument. Her phone was switched off, and her husband was in sweat. The kids were unaware, as they were in their playroom in the basement of the house. She was scared herself. When Tumi eventually showed up, the couple were in their room for a long time, and when they came out, they seemed fine. She looked at them as a miracle. That was the kind of marriage she hoped to get in the nearest future. If it wasn't looking like it, then she wouldn't be going for it. Her flight would land in a little while, so she took a quick cat nap.

THE WEDDING

CHAPTER 7

Carey's wedding was everything any lady would ever want. It was very colorful and beautiful. The decorations in the church and the reception hall were extravagant. The color scheme was peach, gold, and cream. The church and hall were decorated using these colors. The bridesmaids had their beautiful dresses made in peach, and they were holding gold flowers, while the groomsmen had gold suits with peach-colored ties and cream-colored shirts.

Of course, the bride had on a beautiful white flowing dress, and she had her hair made beautifully with a medium-sized diadem. Her natural makeup with silver-colored accessories made her look like a queen. Her flower, peach, gold, and cream in color, complemented her look. As she walked down the aisle with her father, her groom in his cream-colored suit and gold bow tie was looking at her like she was an angel. She was a beauty to behold, one of the things he most cherished about her. His best man whispered in his ear, "Blessed are you with such a beauty." He smiled in return. He had achieved his aim. He was getting married to the woman of his dreams: tall, elegant, respectable famil with good connections. They would make beautiful children together. Most of all, he could be assured she would remain faithful to him and always pray for him "lest he wander away from His presence." He was happy. Elated was the word.

It was time for the vows. They had looked up for examples of promises on the internet, and each of them had picked words to express how they felt for each other, and they also added their own chosen words. Tosin had this to say to his bride:

"Today, surrounded by people who love us, I choose you, Carey, to be my partner. I am proud to be your husband and partner and to join my life with yours. Ever since I set my eyes on you, I have cherished and loved you and your beauty. You are beautiful inside out, specially made for me. I vow to support you, push you, inspire you, and above all love you, for better or worse, in sickness and health, for richer or poorer, as long as we both shall live."

The bride had misty eyes when he finished saying his vows. Then it was her turn.

"I take you as you are, loving who you are now and who you are yet to become. I promise to listen to you and learn from you, to support you and accept your support. I believe in you, Tosin, I know you will make me proud. I will celebrate your triumphs and mourn your losses as though they were my own. I will love you and have faith in your love for me, through all our years and all that life may bring us."

Yeni blinked back a tear when she said, "I know you will make me proud."

The vows were said, and they were pronounced man and wife. The groom kissed the bride, and it was time for the sermon. The pastor called the couple's attention to his sermon. He wanted them to understand what marriage was.

The pastor said marriage was for companionship. For a man and woman to live together in friendship, closeness, togetherness, intimacy and a good rapport. He further said marriage was for procreation, to have children who would be brought up in the way of the Lord. Tosin exchanged looks with his wife and they both smiled. "I know you will give me beautiful children," he whispered and she nodded.

They were still in this mood when the pastor said that the most crucial part of the marriage was that God designed it to be a representation of his love for the church. The church is the bride of Christ. Marriage is based on love between two people, not three. Tosin's grip on his wife's hands turned cold. She felt the change and stared at him. He couldn't meet her eyes; he looked away. The pastor further said that a union with extramarital affairs was heading for the rocks. There would be temptations, but the couple must remember their vows and stay faithful to each other, till death do them apart, just as they had vowed.

The wedding reception was glamorous. The couple's entry was in a grand style. First, it was the bridesmaids and groomsmen that danced in two at a time, a groomsman and a bridesmaid, with the guests clapping and cheering them along, almost everyone was holding out their phones to record the procession. Later on, the best man and best lady did their dance, dancing to a different piece of music. The best man had the opportunity to flirt a little with Yeni, the chief bridesmaid. She didn't like it but couldn't stop it without causing a scene. Then the couple. There was a loud cheer as they danced to the music. They were both excellent dancers, and the guests didn't want them to stop. The couple's second dance was announced after the cutting of the cake. It was another round of beautiful dance steps.

The menu was sumptuous. There were all kinds of food: both African and American. They had jollof rice, fried rice, goat meat, chicken, moin-moin, salad, croaker fish, lasagna, macaroni and cheese, chicken salad, greens made the African way, pounded yam, fruit cocktail, and many more. There were many trays of each food. The guests ate so much, and there were leftovers. The wedding was the talk of the town for a long time afterwards. The bride's father gave the couple a gift of a condo. Their honeymoon was in Paris for six weeks, courtesy of the bride's family.

Susan couldn't attend because she promised Tosin she wouldn't, but she watched most of it live on YouTube from home. She cried so much that her eyes hurt. Susan had learned a big lesson which would remain with her for life. She would never marry. She wished her child would be a boy only because she didn't want a girl who would suffer in the hands of men like she did. She thought she had lived a miserable life. She wished she could keep her promise to let Tosin go. Even if she wanted to, she knew Tosin would come back to her. Would she be able to resist him? Whatever happened, she had decided to stop fighting for him; he was not worth it. She was very hardworking. She would work harder to care for her unborn child and herself, and she would make herself happy. Such is life. She couldn't sleep. She cried so much that her eyes were bloodshot. That was how her aunt met her the next day. She had a lot to say to her to drag her out of her misery.

"You must be insane if you are crying over that boy. It would be best if you were happy he is out of your life. The girl he married is the one tied up to an unstable and promiscuous man. Thank God, you chose not to marry him." Those were her Aunty Joy's words. Susan looked at her and said, "You are getting this wrong. He chose not to marry me and dumped me for her. I guess I'm not good enough for him. He got tired of me after hanging out with me for five years. Five years!"

Joy could not believe it when she found out her niece was four months pregnant by Tosin. She thought she was crazy, and she let her know too.

"I know I'm crazy, Aunty, but I have nothing to do with men, not anymore. I don't want any relationship with them beyond a platonic one. That is why I've decided to be a single parent, At least, I don't have anything to do with men anymore. I am pregnant."

"Well, that's your annoying decision. Let me know how I can help, and please, forget about Tosin. For the sake of your child, keep yourself together in one piece. You know, babies can feel their mom's emotions. Let your baby feel joy and happiness, not sorrow. Train your child right from the womb to be happy. Do it for your baby, not for yourself."

Susan felt better in Joy's presence. Aunty Joy prepared a delicious pot of banga soup with garri and made sure Susan ate some before she left. She cleaned up her kitchen and the living room before she left. They were talking and laughing about matters of interest until one of Joy's children called, and she had to go.

Susan was happy that her aunt visited. She promised to return the visit the following week.

During their conversation, her aunt had said something about "trust in the Lord with all your heart." She searched the internet to find where the words were in the Bible. She typed in "trust in the Lord with all your heart" the Bible verse came up on her search engine as Proverbs 3:5. She ended up reading the whole chapter. She had to admit to herself that she was missing a lot by not reading her Bible daily. She promised herself to make the text her friend again. She missed it. She used to be a good Christian, attending church programs, and listening to the Word of God. Falling in love with Tosin had taken all of that away. She must have been looking for security to fill in the space her parents left after they died in a plane crash six years earlier. Tosin showed up and seemed to be good at making her happy until she found out who he really was. Well, her aunt was right, he had moved on. She should move on, too, with her Bible. It was getting late, and she was getting sleepy. She took a warm shower and got in her cozy pajama dress. She took two pills of Tylenol to dull the pain in her head, said a short prayer, and went straight to sleep. For the first time in a couple of days, she slept soundly.

THE RELATIONSHIP

CHAPTER 8

Yeni and Ralph's relationship seemed to be getting serious. She was getting scared too. She didn't want history to repeat itself. She was not expecting to fall in love with him; she just wanted to give a relationship a try again. She tried to put an end to it. She complained about virtually everything he did and snapped at him for no reason. He wouldn't budge. He kept on being kind to her, never showed a sign of anger. Yeni at first thought he was playing her to get her to fall in love with him, but she found out he wasn't. He proved to her several times that he wasn't playing about loving her.

On this occasion, she was sick, and she went overboard with complaints. She complained about the pain relief medicine he bought for her and about purchasing the wrong blanket. She said he was sitting too close to her; she complained about him not checking on her soon enough; and blamed him for her headache. Ralph simply stood up, picked up his car keys, and left.

Her heart sank just watching him leave. She waited for him to come back, but he didn't. She was restless. She knew she was wrong but didn't know what to do to make things right. She was a brat, and she knew it. Ralph had done nothing but pamper her with love since the relationship started. He didn't show any sign of irresponsibility or promiscuity. Ralph was always there whenever she needed him. He had asked her to come and meet with his family, but she refused. He stopped raising the issue after she had bluntly refused two times. She was unfair to him all because of her previous experience. But he wasn't the cause. Why should she make him suffer for what he didn't do? For all she knew, he might be her "Mr. Right," but that is the problem. Did she really want a "Mr. Right?" She was too scared of what marriage could be like to want to venture into one.

She had always wanted marriage when she was with Alan, but the relationship ended with the destruction of every thought and dream of marriage she might have had. The truth was that she was falling in love again and she feared the unknown. She was sure of one thing, though: she had been unfair to Ralph. She couldn't find anything he did wrong. He was a gentleman to the core -- a Christian too. She thought about what God's mind was about her. She was wrong.

She picked up the phone and dialed her sister, Tumi's, number. "We need to talk, sis; I need some counseling." Tumi knew she was a little bit under the weather, so she decided to drive over to her place. Soon as she walked into her apartment, she said, "This is about Ralph, right?"

Yeni nodded in the affirmative. Tumi moved closer to her and gave her a hug. Yeni held on tightly to her and blinked back a tear. "I'm scared sis, so scared... I think I am falling in love with him, and I just don't know…" She sighed and couldn't finish her sentence. She let two tears slip down her face.

"What are you scared of?" Tumi asked.

"The unknown." She pulled away from her sister and sat down. "Each time I want to open my heart to let him in, it feels like I am entering an unknown destination. I have loved and have been broken. When I love, I love with my whole heart. What if he breaks my heart? I don't want the same terrible thing to happen to me again. How would I handle it if it should?" Tumi sat beside her sister and put one arm over her shoulders.

"Your heart would not be broken a second time," she said. Tumi explained to her sister that the best strategy to use was to trust God. She was to trust God not to let it happen, and not Ralph. She was to pray to God every day to direct her path and release herself to God to do what he would do about her relationship. She should always remember that she is a Christian and conduct herself in like manner.

"You walk upright and wait to see if something looks wrong coming from Ralph. You don't want to blame yourself for frustrating a child of God out of your life. Who knows, this relationship may make your life better. If you ever break up with him, let it not be because you did something wrong; let it be because he was wrong, or your spiritual mind tells you something is dead wrong."

She also told her that the Spirit of God was one. If she would ever take action, she should find a prayer partner. She made a point that she was always available. The last point she made was that marrying Ralph would give her a functional immigration status.

Yeni never liked the idea of getting married to gain immigration status. She wanted marriage for love, but her spirit was relieved after her sister left. She picked up the phone and called Ralph. He didn't answer it. He thought he'd made a wrong choice. If she was unbearable during courtship, how would she be after marriage? He had never shown any girl that much love in his life. He wanted a wife, not a nag. His phone rang again, and he was tempted to answer it, but he didn't. She was probably going to complain again. But when the phone rang for the third time, he hit the green button and left it on speaker but didn't say a word. The first words he heard were: "I'm sorry."

He couldn't believe his ears until she repeated it, and she was ready to say it as many times as possible just to let him know that she really meant it. They had a heart to heart discussion. She told her story. He felt for her and promised her never to intentionally hurt her feelings. He also told her he was ready to play by her rules of the relationship. He would do everything within his power to make her happy. He wanted her to know that he loved her, and he was ready to wait for her to love him back.

Their love blossomed. One of their favorite spots to visit was the movies. They took turns watching each other's type of film. Ralph enjoyed the action movies while Yeni enjoyed the drama. Ralph introduced her to bowling, and she looked forward to their bowling weekends as Ralph enjoyed winning the games. They dined out a lot as these were moments that gave them opportunity to know more about each other.

Yeni cooked excellent dishes. There were times he ate her food, but most times they dined out. Ralph would prefer to see her dressed in her beautiful outfits, sitting opposite him in a luxurious restaurant, ordering and eating and smiling or laughing at his hilarious jokes, rather than imagining her sweating in the kitchen to cook for him.

That could wait until they were married, when he would enjoy eating a warm home-cooked meal after a hard day's work. Lucky him, she was a business owner and she chose when to work. He would eventually make it better for her. He could rent a shop and hire people to work for her or rent out booths to them. That was something he decided to encourage her to do in the nearest future.

They were inseparable, and they were headed to the altar. On a fateful day, they were walking toward Ralph's car after watching a movie when they came face to face with Alan. He had been looking for her to make things right.

She heard someone call her name and she turned back, coming face to face with Alan. He hadn't changed at all. He was standing tall in his blue jeans and blue tee-shirt and a grey Nike sneakers. They stared at each other for a long time until she broke the silence and said "Hello!", and he said "Hello!" Then she turned around, ready to move on. Alan asked to have a word with her, but she refused. When she saw the confused look on Ralph's face, she introduced the two men. Ralph, meet Alan, my ex; Alan, my fiancé, Ralph. They shook hands and Ralph encouraged her to give him audience.

They sat down in a coffee shop close by. Alan was apologetic. He explained to her how his father had insisted on him marrying a girl he had put in the family way when he was seventeen. They got married when they were both eighteen. She was his high school girlfriend, and they were remarkably close friends. His friends had bullied him into having a more intimate relationship with her which had led to the pregnancy. His father, being a clergyman, insisted that he should marry her. He did, but they both decided to finish their education before they would have any more children. He was thinking of divorcing her when he met Yeni. He did not tell her about his marital status because he intended it to end before she would know about it. He did not love his wife, so he said. He never meant to hurt Yeni in any way, but things happened too fast for him to be able to control them. His dad would not allow him to divorce his wife. Instead, he was calling for a traditional wedding. He could only follow his dad's directives because he was his heir. He stood the chance of losing everything if he divorced his wife.

"Why didn't you tell me?" was Yeni's response to the long story.

"If I had told you, you would have left me. I loved you; I still do."

"You loved me?" she giggled. "If you call what you did to me love, then what is hatred?"

He looked away from her, appearing close to tears. "You left me broken in pieces, I was pregnant and jilted." She controlled herself from flaring up.

"Well, if you came to ask for your child, I lost him. I have nothing that is yours with me. Thank you for wasting my time. Have a good day." She got up to leave, but he held her hand, "Yeni, please hear me out." She stared at his hand on her arm and looked at him with disdain. Their eyes met, and he quickly let her go. She sat down.

"I am sorry, Yeni," I was going to cover up my marital status so that I could have you, but it didn't work out my way. I knew about the death of our child. I heard about how hard it was for you. All I can say is that I am sorry. I was selfish, but I was trying to be happy." He told her he did not love his wife. He had postponed their traditional wedding too many times but could no longer do so because his dad had terminal cancer and had limited time to live. He had to make him happy. He wanted her to forgive him.

Yeni looked at him for a long time and sighed. "I am happy and relieved that I have the opportunity of speaking with you today. You used to be a heavy burden in my heart. There were days and nights I yearned for you, days and nights I blamed you or myself for the hurt I went through, but I am now free of hurt and shame and condemnation. I am happy and blessed. I want you to know that I have forgiven you from the bottom of my heart, I have. Find a place in your heart to love your wife. I love my fiancé very much, and he loves me too."

She glanced at Ralph where he was seated a couple of seats away from them. They winked at each other, exchanging smiles. "The Bible does not support divorce; pray for the grace to love your wife." She was done and stretched out her hand to him for a handshake. He took it reluctantly, "Nice talking with you," she said as she shook his hand in a firm grip. "I'm glad we had this conversation." She walked over to Ralph's table and sat across the table from him.

"Did you order my coffee?" she asked. "Yes, I did, along with a muffin," he answered.

THE MEETING

CHAPTER 9

usan was getting big. Her face was swollen. Her nose was bigger. She had added several pounds. Her whole body was strange to her because she was seven months pregnant. She was lonely except for Aunty Joy's frequent visits. What would she have done without her? Nothing was the answer. She gave her all kinds of support: spiritual, physical, emotional, name it. She was there for her. She decided to take a walk today just as Aunty Joy had suggested but she changed her mind about the trail and decided to go to the store instead.

She went to the Giant for some groceries. She was happy to find some fruit and food items she had been longing for. She found coconut, pawpaw, and grapefruit. She also found an African-made bread, which she put in her cart with delight. She was thinking of the pleasure in her taste buds as she would munch on the roll, when a pile of big fresh plantains came into view. It was across the aisle from the African bread. As she pushed her cart excitedly to the plantains, she saw someone who looked familiar. She looked closely, and it was Carey, Tosin's wife.

She turned her cart away and quickly walked toward another aisle. What was Carey doing in her neighborhood? She pushed her cart around for some minutes and then headed back to the plantains. There was no one there. She was joyfully making her choice when Carey walked back to the plantains right beside her, and she was on the phone. As Susan looked up, their eyes locked. There was silence. Within the silence was a question on Carey's face, then a recognition, and then a knowing look.

"Hello!," Carey broke the silence.

"Hello!," Susan said and tried to walk away.

"Susan, right?"

"Yes."

"How have you been?"

"I've been good, and you?"

"I am fine. Congratulations," Carey said, pointing to Susan's protruded tummy.

"Thank you."

"I am happy you moved on." Susan smiled in return.

"Wishing you a safe delivery."

"Thank you."

"You have a good evening," Carey said. Before she could walk away, Susan said, "I am sorry for everything."

"For what?" Carey asked. "You did nothing to me. I am just happy you moved on with your life. I am sure you're in love with your...," she looked at her hand and saw no ring "...husband."

Susan followed her eyes and smiled; "You don't want to know."

With that, she walked away. Carey couldn't keep her mind off the conversation she had with Susan at the store. It kept coming to her mind and she did not know why. She had nobody to talk to. Tosin was out of town on business, Yeni was on a date with Ralph, and she barely answered her calls. She had no other friend. It was a cold night, so she curled up in bed with a hot cup of cocoa, watching a movie. She dozed off only to wake up thirty minutes later from a disturbing dream. In her dream, she saw Susan wearing Tosin's new tuxedo, the grey one she bought for him for his birthday. She moved closer to her and questioned her with her eyes. Susan looked elated with her beaming smiles, then, Carey challenged her with words, she wanted to know why she was wearing her husband's clothes. Susan stared at her for an extended time before giving her a reply. "You can figure it out." She walked away with smiles, leaving Carey with an astonished look.

She woke up with a start. What a dream! What could it mean? She called Yeni again. This time, she answered the call with a drowsy response, "I'll call you in the morning, girlfriend."

She felt like throwing the phone against the wall. "Alright," she said to herself, "I need to calm down, everything will be alright." With that, she turned back to the TV just in time for LMN to begin a new movie. She used the cinema to block the rising anxiety within her. It helped. The film was entertaining, but she couldn't sleep. She had barely dozed off in the early hours of the morning when Tosin called. Something came up, and he had to stay longer than he thought he would. He'd be back in two days. The thought of what came up kept sleep away from her. She finally went to sleep after she had had a warm glass of milk. She woke up with a fever. She took two Tylenol pills, turned her phone off, and went back to sleep. She woke up an hour later with a pang of hunger. She wondered what to eat. Moin-moin was her choice, her leftover dinner. She could make some custard and have a good meal. That she did. The meal was so good she wanted more, but she decided to save the rest for later.

After washing the dishes, she decided to do laundry. The fragrance from the laundry soap gave her instant nausea. Before she could figure out why, she had started vomiting. All the good food went down the drain. That was how she spent her day. She vomited all day until there was nothing left to vomit. She only remembered to turn her phone on in the late afternoon. Yeni had left two messages. She was eagerly looking forward to one from her husband, but there was none. She decided not to call him; she called Yeni. She laughed when Carey said she had been vomiting.

"You need a pregnancy test, girl. Go get one and call me back." That was it! She was pregnant! At last, she was! She'd been anxious about it for the past five months since she'd been married. She needed to be sure. She dragged her weak body to the car but felt too weak to drive. She called Uber.

Tosin had to change his plans about going home after work on that fateful day because Susan had texted him to say she saw his wife. He had been avoiding her since he got married but had been sending her money. Tosin was relieved of the tension when he realized she wasn't pressuring him into paying her visits. There was no communication between them except the short thank you messages he received from her each time he sent her money. He called her to ask what was going on. She said it was nothing and didn't bother to give him further information. He decided to pay her a visit. She did not say anything to stop him from visiting her, probably because she did not think he would. He still took a flight to Texas. He just didn't go home; he went straight to Susan's house. He had some problems figuring out what to tell his wife. He was supposed to be back in Texas with his wife after three days on the business trip, but he had to see Susan. He ended up telling her something came up and was surprised when she did not ask him what it was. She was probably tired from grocery shopping. She was always shopping. Susan was surprised to see him. She had thought he would call her to talk about the information she had given him about his wife, but she was wrong. He was right there on her front porch!

"Hello... Susan..." Susan stared at him as if he was a ghost. She was dumbfounded. Is this the same Tosin or his spirit?

"Can I come in?" she made way for him to come in, and motioned for him to sit down. Then she found her voice.

"Why are you here?"

"To see you... and the baby," he said, stammering the word baby and pointing at her stomach. "You look so different," he said, looking at her intensely.

"I guess I now look ugly to you," she said sarcastically.

"Actually, more beautiful," he said with the same soft voice that had always made her forget her worries. And she did. She forgot about her promise to stop loving him. She was looking at the love of her life, the father of her unborn child. She had missed him so much. How could she ever forget him? Impossible. She offered to get him something to eat. She had some bitter leaf soup in the freezer that her aunt had prepared the last time she visited. All she had to do was defrost it in the microwave and make some garri to go along with it. She set out the food and had a bottle of sparkling cider to go with it. They sat down together to eat, at first in silence and then he broke the silence.

"This is delicious, you still cook good soups." She responded with a smile. She wanted to ask him if his wife didn't cook for him, but the moment meant so much to her she didn't want to mess around with it by mentioning his wife's name.

"Have you ever thought about being a professional cook? You can open an African cuisine…"

"Aunty Joy made the soup, I didn't."

"Ooh, I see."

"I have not been able to cook or eat very well for months. I had to quit my job. Aunty Joy has been accommodating. She cooks, shops, cleans, and checks on me regularly." She told him how she had been sick and miserable for months. She was just getting better. She hadn't eaten well for so long. She concluded by saying his presence must have done the magic. Only then, a phone call came through for Tosin from the doctor's office. He ignored it and put his phone on silent mode. He continued listening to Susan. When she was finished talking, he held her hand and promised to never leave her by herself again. She told him that was a lie because he was married to someone else. He responded by saying she was his responsibility because he had impregnated her. At that moment, she wanted to tell him about how she met his wife at the store, but he motioned for her to stop.

"I love you, Susan," he said, "I had thought keeping away from you would take your love out of my heart, but I was mistaken. I still love you despite the circumstances. I still do. "

"What are we going to do about it?" she asked.

"We keep on loving each other. Period! I am spending the night here, to start with."

At that moment, Susan forgot all the promises she made to herself and her aunt to stay away from him. She ignored the prayer of forgiveness of sins and forgot about seeing Carey and apologizing to her. She was looking at the man holding her hand and professing his love for her. She tried to avoid locking eyes with him. She decided to withdraw her hands from his firm grasp but couldn't. He whispered the words, "I'm sorry."

She looked into his eyes, and tears rolled down her face. She remembered the lonely nights, the nightmares, the pain of suffering without him. She couldn't resist his love; she had to accept him again. Then he went on his knees. Now, that was too much. He was begging for her love. She had to take it since he was giving it on a platter of gold.

He fulfilled his promise of spending the night with her. It was a Friday, and so he decided to stay for the weekend. He didn't check his phone until noon the next day, and he found out that his wife had called him ten times. He called back. She wanted to know why he hadn't answered his phone. He said he had left it in the hotel room before he went for an all-night meeting. He didn't realize he had left it behind until this morning. He had just found it in the corner of his bed, and it was on silent. That was the beginning of the lies. The lies came so quickly, and they always worked. He lived his double life with no remorse. He sometimes joked about it as what he was made for.

Carey told him she was at the hospital. He was shocked to hear the news but was relieved to hear she was okay, and he faked excitement when she told him she was pregnant. Tosin was confused. He had two grown women pregnant! "This is insanity," so he thought. He told her he would be on the next flight home. Susan gave him a questioning look.

"Breaking your promise already?"

"Not at all. I am staying for the weekend. Let Carey be on the lookout for me."

Luckily for Susan, Aunty Joy called to say she would not be able to visit as promised; she had an urgent meeting to attend. Susan was elated! She didn't have to worry about explaining to Aunty Joy about her reunion with Tosin. He was all hers; this time, she wouldn't let him slip out of her hands. He called Carey and told her the next available flight to Houston was not until 5:00 p.m. on Sunday. She believed him. Tosin knew his wife was very sensitive to smell, so he decided to do laundry before he left.

He made sure he was wearing a washed shirt and a clean pair of pants on his way home. He got back around 9:00 p.m.

HE DOUBLE GAME

CHAPTER 10

Tosin was a consumer products operations manager working for Bosling Whole Foods in Houston, Texas. The company had been doing extremely well since he joined the administrative team. His immediate supervisor, the owner of the company, had entrusted the success of the new company in New York to him. He was supposed to be gone for three days. He had left on a Tuesday and was supposed to be back Thursday night or Friday morning and have the rest of the day off, but he had told his wife he wouldn't be back till Friday night and had to change the story to Sunday night. He hoped she didn't doubt him.

He thought it was a coincidence that his job now required him to be in New York every month for the next few months or until the new company over there was doing well enough to be left alone. He thought this would be an excellent opportunity for him to spend some days with Susan. Just as he was concluding in his mind to always stop by at Susan's each time he had to go to New York, he thought about someone who knew his wife spotting him and snitching on him. Carey's sister-in-law lived not far away from Susan's place. Carey was probably visiting her when she stopped at the store where she saw Susan. He was sure that was the case. The distance of a little over an hour's drive was too much for his wife to make just because she wanted groceries. Only a few minutes from where they resided, several grocery stores were her favorite spots for fresh fruits. He would wait to hear the story she had to tell about meeting Susan at the store. He prepared himself for a perfect act. He wasn't trying to lose Carey, and he wasn't letting go of Susan either. He just had to be smart!

Speaking of being smart, he had to think of moving Susan farther away from Carey. That shouldn't be a problem for him since he had rented the apartment for her and was still responsible for paying the rent. He would talk to her about it the next time he visited. Then he thought about why he didn't marry Susan in the first place. Why did he decide to let go of her to marry another woman? Another woman? Did he just refer to his legally married wife as another woman? Something was wrong with him but he couldn't place what it was.

His mind went back to how he had met Susan. It was on a rainy day. He was driving home from work, and it was getting dark. He slowed down as the green light turned yellow and he came to a complete stop just as the light turned red. He remembered he had seen an adult in a movie play the "red light stop and green light go" game with a group of students. He smiled as the adult's delightful smile came back to his memory. One day, he would have children of his own. He would marry a beautiful African lady and have up to six children. He smiled again at the thought of it. Just before the light turned green, he noticed a lovely lady trying to cover herself with a scarf to avoid getting wet. He shook his head with regret. "That definitely would be one of my people. Didn't she see the weather forecast?" He asked no one in particular. Rain was in the forecast for that day, and anyone stepping outdoors should be prepared for the storm by having an umbrella with them. The light turned green, and he drove ahead, pulling over to the right lane until he stopped in front of the lady getting wet. He rolled down the side window and said,

"Hello, sweetie." She walked away from him. He drove closer to her.

"It's obvious you need a ride. You may hop in, and I'll drop you home." Susan looked at him like she was having second thoughts.

"I don't bite people. Just trying to help. Where are you going?"

"Hillcrest Road," she said with a straight face.

"Hop in," he said. With a little reluctance, Susan did.

"Thank you," she said without leaving a hint in her attitude or tone of voice that she meant it. Tosin headed toward Hillcrest Road, and they were silent for a few minutes until he broke the silence by asking her where she was from. She told him she was from Imo state in Nigeria, and he was happy she was from

Nigeria because that was where he was from. But he was from Oyo State. That was the beginning of a chat that lasted for the fifteen-minute drive. When he eventually pulled up in front of her apartment building, they were talking and laughing like old friends. Only then did he ask for her name and phone number. She knew she would love to see him again, so she agreed to a lunch date with him for the next day. He reached in the back seat of his car and offered her an umbrella.

"Rain is in the forecast all week. You will need an umbrella." She looked at the quizzical look on his face and burst out laughing.

"Really? I had an umbrella today. I gave it to an elderly co-worker of mine whose car broke down and couldn't drive home. I always have one."

"That was nice of you, but now you do not have one; you can have mine," he said, insisting she take the umbrella.

"I don't need it. I have another one in my room. Thank you." She got out of his car, closed the door, and walked away swiftly.

"See you tomorrow!" he yelled out behind her." She turned around and waved at him.

"I hope she shows up," he said to himself. "I like her."

At that time, Susan was living with her Aunt Joy. She had a husband and five children: two boys and three girls. Susan kept her belongings in a corner in the girls' room. The couch in the living room was her bed at night. She was working in a convenience store on Preston Road, Houston, Texas, and what she earned was barely enough for her to save enough to get her own apartment. Her aunt would have helped her to secure a place if she had had the money. Susan was saving some money but wasn't sure exactly when there would be enough, as there were bills for her to pay and contribute to the upkeep of the house. She also had to send money to her family back in Imo State.

It wasn't easy for her to save, but she kept on hoping she would find a second job to be able to save enough. She was tired of sleeping on the couch. She also overheard Aunt Joy's husband complaining about her stay with them. Her sweet aunt had apologized on her behalf and requested that he give her more time. She said she was working on moving out to her own place. As Susan walked away from Tosin's car that night, she thought about what she'd said about her room. She really longed to have a room to herself. She knew her dream would come to pass one day. Walking into the house, she found the whole family sitting at the dining room table, eating dinner. She greeted them warmly and walked in briskly to change from her wet clothes before the girls would be ready for their room. She had barely finished dressing up when her aunt knocked and walked into the room. Her message was simple. Susan was given two months to get herself a place to live. They'd been generous enough by allowing her to stay with them for the past three months.

That night, she barely slept. It was enough to worry that she didn't have enough money. How would she find a place to live in? She had asked her aunt to help her look around, but she said she had to find a way by herself. She was old enough to know what to do, "This is America, nobody will live your life for you," were her cold words.

Susan wasn't asking anyone to live her life for her; she only needed assistance. She had been around for less than a year. She didn't know how to go about getting an apartment to live in. She thought about her aunt's words once again, and she concluded those words were a repeated version of her husband's words. She had heard him say those words a couple of times before.

The lunch date was perfect. They enjoyed each other's company. By the end of the dinner, Tosin felt like he had known her for ages. She told him everything about herself leaving out the fact that she slept in the living room. She didn't want to tell him what hurt the most on a first date. They had an excellent time. That was it. He didn't have to formally ask her to date him; they just got closer each time. The relationship blossomed, and they went everywhere together. She had to eventually tell him about her predicament, and he surprised her by renting a one-bedroom apartment for her. He paid the rent monthly. She was more than grateful. That was it. She viewed him as her husband. He was everything to her; she could barely do anything without bringing him into it. She was head over heels in love with him. Then came the pregnancies, three precisely. He had requested she get rid of them until he was ready for marriage. Although it hurt her to have to do the abortions, the idea coming from him made it perfect for her. She thought she had found the right man to be married to.

Susan did not play hard to get, but Carey did. That got his attention. Carey carried herself with her respect and dignity. She didn't care if he was there or not; she went about her business. Then he found out she was from a wealthy family. He had always wanted to be married to a girl brought up with a silver spoon. That was Carey. Tosin was from a poor family but was able to work hard enough to be comfortable. That was not enough. If he had a wife from an influential family that would complement his humble background, that would be a surety that he would never return to poverty.

Poverty stinks. He never wanted it around him. He also found out that Carey was a good Christian. She went to church regularly, and she was prayerful. He was stunned when she told him she was going to pray about him asking her out before she could say yes. He had expected her to say he should give her some time, but pray? He did not expect that. That also added to his determination to marry into her wealthy and prominent family with its solid Christian background. He didn't need to seek any further; he had found his soul mate. He was overjoyed when she said yes to his proposal. He worshipped her, more out of respect than of love, but thought it was love. He was also a Christian but didn't go to church regularly. He believed Jesus is the Lord, and he believed in miracles. He got closer to God when he was dating Carey, and he was surprised when she told him she had a revelation about him warming up to God. That was true.

Coming back from his reverie, he thought about his weekend with Susan that had revealed to him whom he loved. He should have left Carey alone, but he didn't. Well, he would show the world that he could eat his cake and have it too. He was determined to live the double life if Susan could cope with it and if Carey never found out about it. He would make himself the sweetest husband ever. Every woman loves to be pampered. Now that she was pregnant, Tosin promised himself to make her as comfortable as ever. He used to keep chains of girlfriends, and he was able to manage them. Managing mature women shouldn't be a problem now.

THE PREPARATION

CHAPTER 11

I t was a spring morning. The temperature was in the upper 50s and it felt so good with the sun rising beautifully. Yeni couldn't resist the view from her window. She decided to take a walk down the street. She had on a sweater jacket on the top of her grey T-shirt. She was wearing a pair of blue jeans with blue sneakers. She had no makeup; it was 7:00 a.m., too early for that. Her first client for the day was not due to come in until 10:00 a.m. She walked through Chesapeake Street and turned onto 4th street. She told herself she would turn back when she got to the firehouse. She saw people walking and students catching a bus to school. Some were waiting on the bus and traffic was building up. She was strolling and enjoying the cool morning breeze.

The breeze blew her hair across her face, and she pulled it behind her ear. She enjoyed the feel. She was blessed with extra-long hair; most African women's hair is not as long. Her hair was permed, and if left loose as it rested beyond her shoulders. Ironically, she got her long hair from her father, not her mother. Her sister, Tumi, had the short hair she got from their mother. She smiled at the thought of how she used to tease her about her short hair.

That thought about Tumi came at the right time. She was a perfect sister. She owed a lot to her. She was responsible for getting her a hair salon place -- that made her an entrepreneur. She set her own schedule, and she had enough clients and made enough to pay her bills.

The room was big enough to have two or more people braiding hair at the same time, but she only had one booth set up. She was expecting the young girl to come for an interview in a couple of days. She had to be ready. She needed some time to pray about it and to get more furniture. She'd been doing this alone without a hitch. She had to be sure in her spirit mind that she would be hiring the right hand. She didn't want any form of headache in any way.

The hair salon she had worked in before she had her own business had taught her enough. The girls there were sneaky; they told stories about one another for favors. The owner got jealous of the other girls when they made a lot of money, and she tried to cheat them out of their pay. Each braider got half of the payment; the owner most times took more than was necessary. Therefore, there was always chaos. A lot of times, she had to settle quarrels.

And there were snitches. When the owner was not there, some girls tried to do some hair without recording it in the book, and they got snitched on. It was just too much for her. The beauty of it was that none of these was open to customers. She could have re-named the place "Island Unrest" instead of "Island Braiders."

Well, that chapter of her life was over, never to return. Her life had been moving in stages. Wasn't God faithful? Couldn't thank him enough.

Her wedding was fast approaching and it felt like a dream. For real? Yeni was getting married? After all she went through, it was indeed a favor and a second chance from God. She prayed she would not flaunt the opportunity.

She had decided to have a quiet wedding and was happy that Ralph agreed with her. They were going to have a few of their family members and friends present and they would have an extended honeymoon, the location of which had not been agreed on. The place would be a surprise for her. Ralph was good at surprising her, but she was eager to unravel the surprise. He also said their home would be a surprise. When she argued about wanting to set up her own home the way she wanted it, he had asked her to make a list of what she wished. What an amazing God that makes amazing things happen!

She started imagining how she would look in her wedding gown. She had to choose a style first, she told herself. Tumi had sent her a link to a wedding website. The website had everything and she only had to choose. She didn't have to pay for anything. If Ralph wasn't paying, Tumi was. "It feels so good to be loved," she whispered to herself. Yeni turned around quickly to see if anyone heard her. No one seemed to know she was talking. An old man was struggling with his car keys beside his car. A middle-aged man was walking his dog on the other side of the street, and there was a metro bus just approaching the bus stop. No one seemed to have heard her; everyone minded their business. She really wished she could stand on the top of a mountain and yell out, "I am loved!"

She had turned back toward her residence on Atlantic Street when her phone rang. She knew who it was before she checked. It was Ralph calling to say good morning, and to remind her to get on the wedding website and choose colors and styles. She promised to. When she got off the phone with Ralph, she gave Carey a quick call.

"Hello, girlfriend," Carey said sleepily.

"Don't tell me you're just waking up?" Yeni asked, surprised.

"Yes…" was the sleepy reply.

"You're not going to work?"

"I resume work from my sick leave tomorrow."

"You're sick again?"

"Not really, I just needed some time off, and made my doctor write me a sick leave letter."

"Good to know you're okay."

"Yeah, I'm okay, just getting tired too often."

"Girl, don't be lazy! You're not that big, are you?"

"Yes, I am. I am over 185 pounds now."

"OMG! I need to see you. Send me a picture."

"You don't want to see my puffy eyes."

"No, I don't want to but I know you're still beautiful."

"I don't believe you. You need to see me before jumping to conclusions. I am too big to be beautiful. Enough about me, though; let's talk about you. What are you up to?"

"My wedding. I'll need your help with choosing colors and styles and, you know, a lot of things."

"When are you coming over?" Carey asked, excited.

"I thought we could do it over the phone."

"No way! You must come. We need to sit together over this to make it work."

"I need to check my schedule to be sure of when I can come. I am booked throughout the month."

"You need some time off; get some help!"

"Hey girl, stop yelling at me. It's not that serious," Yeni said, exhausted.

"Yes, it is. It's easiest to come next weekend, Hubby's weekend to go out of town. I can enjoy your company."

"It's a date! I'll get help like you said. See you then!"

"That's my girl."

It was easy for her to go. All she had to do was allow the new apprentice to start earlier than she scheduled her to. She was good too. That was a blessing. They had an agreement on how she would get paid, and Yeni was free. She would have enough time to plan her wedding. It was four months away. She hoped Carey would be able to make it.

There was a lot to choose from. She bought different magazines and found another site she stumbled on, aside from the one Tumi sent to her. Then she had a magazine that her mom had mailed her all the way from Nigeria! Isn't that something! Everyone around her was excited for her. Her parents were waiting on her to send their invitation cards that they could take to the embassy. Now that she was really planning, it was looking real.

She was about to become a Mrs. She was also about to become a legal resident in the United States of America. Two prayer points answered in one. One thing she thought of not leaving out was prayers. She had weekly prayer sessions with Ralph. They chose two days in the week to fast and pray. Their prayer points ranged from the preparation to the wedding day, and the married life afterwards. They also included journey mercies for their friends and family members that would be in attendance. Ralph deposited a sum of $15,000 into her account for the preparation. He had paid for the hall and the decorations. Ralph was waiting for Yeni to decide on the menu for the day. He would have also made payments, but a caterer was already handy. Ralph was moving very quickly. He was ready to be a husband and a father. He wished Yeni would show more excitement and move more quickly with the planning.

On a second thought, he said to himself, "Moving faster with the planning wouldn't make the day come sooner;it would only make it to, hopefully, be on point." His family members were excited too. They were giving him all the support he needed. His parents were ready to spend as much as was required. They even promised them a home in Maryland. That was why he kept it as a surprise from his wife-to-be. He only gave his mom a list of the items and colors she wanted. He knew she would love the house. He also had a plan to buy her a car. She wasn't driving now, but she could drive. The brand-new car would be his gift to her. He had a lot of surprises. They would be going to Paris for their honeymoon. Only the best was good enough for the love of his life. She deserved happiness and pampering. If only Yeni knew how much he loved her...

He had chosen his brother as his best man, and four of his colleagues as his groomsmen. He wondered who Yeni would choose as the chief bridesmaid or the bridesmaids. Well, her trip to Carey should answer all the questions. He did not tell her about the groomsmen. He knew already that she would be against it, but notwithstanding, it was his wedding too! He was right; she pulled up an argument when he mentioned it.

"Four groomsmen? What do you need them for?" she said exasperated.

"Groomsmen," he said as a matter of fact, "that's what I need them for."

"Are they included in our list of guests?" she said, lowering her voice.

"No."

"So, what happened to a quiet wedding?" she asked, still a bit petulant.

"Nothing. Thirty plus four becomes thirty-four guests. The wedding is still quiet."

"Quiet? With an extra four people? No, Ralph, what are you doing?"

"I am inviting guests to my wedding. I am making it colorful."

"It's my wedding!" she said with emphasis.

"Mine too, bae, and I am excited about it. I want the whole world to know that I am getting married to the most beautiful woman in the world." He stopped to wink at her, and then continued in a whisper, "I want to show you off to the world."

Her angry face slowly changed to a smile.

"You're impossible, Ralph. Can't I win one argument with you? You always have something to say to win our arguments."

"Can't beat that, bae. Plus, I really meant what I said. You are the excitement about the wedding -- not the guests, or the food or the clothes. It's you I want, not the ceremony. But I want a beautiful ceremony for us to enjoy and to cherish afterward."

She was silent after she heard those words from the man she would be married to in less than four months. She had no doubt in her mind that she was making the right decision.

Justin, Ralph's brother, cleared his throat to remind them that he was in the next room. He walked into the family living room where they were, and he told his brother he would be most grateful to God if he could find the love of his life like Ralph did. He welcomed Yeni into the family.

Justin thought Yeni was a rare woman. He had never heard of a woman who did not like a big wedding. This was his first time. To him, it meant she had little pleasure in the things of this world. She would be good with money management. She was the best for her brother. He glanced at the poem on his phone; he had taken a picture of it when he went into his brother's room the day before. It was on his lampstand.

Black
Black is beautiful
Black is bold
Black is blessed

Blossoming in bliss

Black is radiant
Under the bright shining sun
Black is gorgeous
Brighter than light

Black head is brighter than light
Black mind is more transparent than water
Black-saved soul is pointing to heaven
Within the deepest black

Life is rebirth
Woman of color
Shining like the sun
Man of color radiating like the moon
The color makes the difference.

Ralph said he was going to replace every "Black" in the poem with "Yeni". He wanted Justin to help print it into a card and give it to his future wife. Justin thought the height of their love was limitless.

Well, the argument about a quiet wedding was ended with a new decision to make it big after she heard her sister, Tumi, talking on the phone with her friend about "aso ebi". Tumi actually wanted her friends to wear the same outfit on her wedding day. She knew already what Tumi's response would be if she had challenged her about it. She would have said she was inviting her friends to her only sister's wedding.

Her weekend with Carey was excellent. Carey was in a unique spirit about the wedding, just as everyone around her was. She wasn't thinking about "aso ebi" like her sister was, but she named girls who would be her escort at the wedding. She also suggested someone as a chief bridesmaid. Yeni wouldn't agree to that, "You will have had your baby by then. You can still be my chief bridesmaid. You're my best, and I would love for you to be there for me."

"I would have loved to be there for you, but I am married, and I would be breastfeeding. It's not going to be easy. I am fat now and might even be bigger then. I may not be able to move around and do everything needed to be done. I will need to pump breast milk, keep it clean, cool, and clean up really good afterward. And what if I am not even strong enough to run around, or I get hungry at the wrong time, or breast milk chooses the wrong time to flow? Or…"

"It's fine," Yeni cut her short, "I'll use someone else."

"I am so sorry, Sugar…", Carey said sincerely, but Yeni rolled her eyes at her. "Okay, Yeni, I'll give you the cutest chief bridesmaid ever! You would love her!" Carey said with a big smile. Yeni didn't want that; she wanted to choose her own chief bridesmaid.

They shopped through the wedding site together and were able to select colors and make reservations for a lot of items.

They created a wedding website, and they began a guest list. They decided that the guest list would be strictly by RSVP. She sent the website link to her husband-to-be and her sister. She was surprised to see that, within a day, sixty people were already on the RSVP list! She had not invited anyone at all; the guest lists were coming in from Ralph and Tumi. Amazing!

She arrived at Carey's on a Friday, and by the time she was leaving on Sunday morning, she noticed that Tosin was calling for the first time since her arrival. She also noticed that her friend's countenance was sad while receiving the message. There were no endearments in her responses. All she had was "Ok, thank you. See you soon. Bye." Carey also went into a quiet mood after receiving the call. Something was wrong.

"Are you okay?" Yeni asked, expecting to hear her say yes, and then cover up with sweet words, but instead, she replied, "No," with emphasis.

"Something is wrong with my marriage but I don't understand what it is."

"Do you feel like talking about it?" Yeni asked with caution.

"I am already talking about it. I don't understand him anymore. I think he is too friendly. He is so sweet toward me sometimes that I think he is not real. At the same time, I feel like he's not there. He buys random gifts, and uses endearments. He is just extra-natural. I don't understand him anymore," Carey said really worried. Yeni burst out laughing.

"I am talking about something that hurts me badly, and you're laughing? This is not a joke!"

Yeni stopped laughing when she saw the look on her friend's face.

"I'm sorry. I was laughing because I cannot see what you see Don't you think Tosin just loves you more and he's trying to show it to you?"

"No, Yeni, I think he is trying to hide something!" she exclaimed, relieved to let it out at last.

"What do you think he might be hiding?" she asked, concerned.

"I don't know, I only pray it's nothing about his job. I will have to quit mine soon because of the baby. I've been in and out of the hospital, and my doctor has suggested bed rest. She would insist on bed rest if I land in there again before my due date. That is, if it's not my regular checkup day."

"But you said he's out of town on his job. Don't you think that should mean he's doing well?"

"Maybe. I don't know what to believe. "

"Have you talked to him about this?"

"No, I haven't," she replied. "I seriously think my husband is hiding something."

"Have you prayed about it?" Yeni asked, "because if it worries you this much, you should."

"I will pray about it. Thank you."

"And also talk to him about it," Yeni encouraged.

"I will, Yeni. I am feeling better already. That's why you're always the best."

She gave her friend a big hug, and they hugged as old friends.

FAMILIES

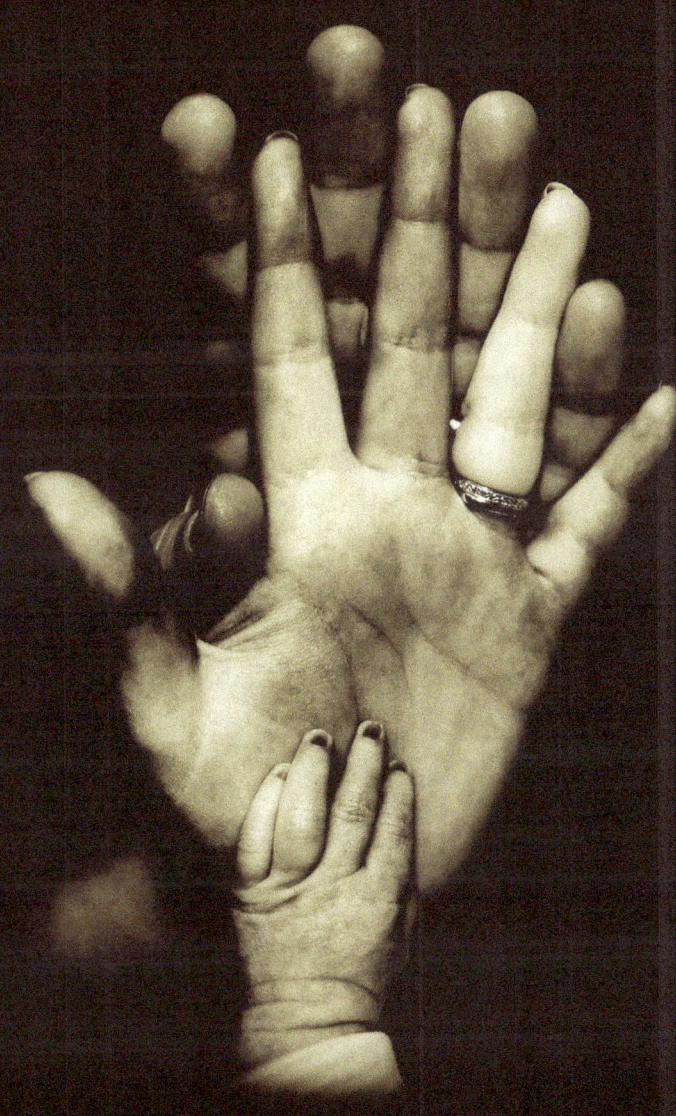

CHAPTER 12

Paul Nwachukwu was from a very humble background. His father was a small-scale farmer in a small village in Anambra State, Nigeria. His mother was a petty trader. He was born into a family of six children. He was the only son and the last born of the family; therefore, he was sent to school. His father struggled to send him to school. He was always the laughingstock of his classmates in every school environment he went to, either because he was so late in paying his fees or because his uniform was too small or ripped in visible places.

Several times, he had cried his way home from school either for non-payment of tuition or because he was being bullied. He vowed never to let any of his children go through the same thing he went through. He promised to work hard and make more than enough to cater to his family. This he did. When he met his wife, he wasn't ready for marriage, and he was happy because she was prepared to wait for him. When he got the opportunity to go to America, he was elated, and he quickly decided to have a wedding so that his wife could go with him. He made sure they did not have any children until he got a stable job and an apartment of their own. They were not ready to have children for the first two years and had to wait another two years before his wife became pregnant. So, four years passed slowly by until they had their first child, Raphael Nwachukwu.

Raphael, later often called Ralph, was the first of two sons the couple had. When the boys were growing up, they had the best of everything they needed. Paul made sure they were never in any form of government assistance program To him, that was a sign of poverty. He detested anything associated with poverty. Paul worked very hard. He became a medical doctor and his wife, a nurse practitioner. He became a doctor not out of interest but out of his quest for unlimited wealth. It paid off He was good at his job, and he got paid good money. Aside from being a medical doctor, he was also a businessman. He was shipping and selling cars in Nigeria. He was also building and renting out apartment buildings both in America and in Nigeria.

By the time his two sons were grown-up boys, he had made a lot of money. He had no more worries about poverty. His sons were up-and-coming; they had good jobs, and one of them was about to be married. It was his time to celebrate!

He and his wife decided to spend as much as possible on the wedding because they wanted their son to feel loved. They wanted him to enjoy the affluence they had labored to build in donkey's years. What exactly is the purpose of working hard to build wealth if not for your offspring to enjoy the splendor?

They invited friends and families from home and abroad. They belonged to the Igbo community of the

Christian Association in Maryland. The association was ready to give their support in any way that was required of them. They were going to beautify the wedding ceremony with their traditional outfit: the ladies would wear their plain wrappers with elegant blouses, usually made of wax and guipure materials, and the men would wear their traditional attire called Isiagu. Ralph's family was ready to help the couple start on a solid foundation of wealth and affluence; they were giving them a house as a wedding gift.

The groom's mom would furnish the home to the taste of her daughter-in-law to be. Money was not an issue. Her sources of income were numerous, ranging from a chain of businesses, as well as three prominent boutiques in Nigeria. She inherited houses and millions of naira from her late father. She had taken Yeni as the daughter she never had. Desiring that Yeni always feel welcome, she did her best to make her comfortable. She wanted her to feel welcome. She gave her an Igbo name, Adamma, which means "beautiful girl".

The family was happy. Paul was elated because his dream had come true. He was able to give his children what his parents couldn't give him: comfortability and respect. Paul was most grateful to his parents for struggling to send him to school, because this was the foundation that he built on. He was also thankful to God, who had given him the life and good health to be able to achieve his dreams. Paul thought about a thanksgiving gift to God. He was going to discuss it with his wife; she always had great ideas about things like that.

Omoyeni's family was not left out. They had their trip to Washington, DC planned. They were going to the wedding with their friends. Ten people would be traveling with them. Two family friends and eight family members. They had their beautifully designed "aso ebi" and beautiful gifts for the couple. Yeni's mom was ready for her daughter. She bought some food items she thought she would need and other items that Tumi had asked her for. She was excited. At last, her daughter was getting married and had finally made her proud. God had taken the shame away. She was from a polygamous home; her dad was married to three wives, and each wife had five children It was like a competition. Her mom was the third wife, and because she was learned, it reflected in her upbringing. Her siblings had always envied her success in life. Yeni's mom was a renowned lawyer by profession. She was married to an accountant, and they had a small, charming family. The two daughters were okay with that. Their first daughter studied in the U.S. and decided to remain there.

Their second daughter, Omoyeni, almost made them proud in the end, though they couldn't swallow what she did. Getting pregnant during her National

Youth Service year was a hard blow. How could a child come back from service year pregnant and without a responsible man for the pregnancy? It was a shame to them. Her polygamous family finally had the opportunity to laugh at her -- behind her back. No one could confront her with mockery. They were all whispers that echoed in her head. The church wasn't easy on them either. People whispered and said things they shouldn't know. They intentionally asked after Omoyeni to check if she was in good health. Hypocrisy was everywhere. Silent and verbal condemnation was constant. It seemed as if people were always looking forward to another person's downfall. But a lot of people became sympathetic when she lost her baby. It wasn't something they could hide because it was evident that she was pregnant. She was seven months pregnant before she had the still birth.

They told everyone about the wedding, they gave out invitation cards. The parents wanted people to know that Omoyeni was getting married, even if they would not be able to attend. They assured them that the wedding would be live on YouTube and Facebook people in Nigeria could watch. The wedding was held on a Saturday, they arrived at their hotel rooms the Wednesday before the event. Their suitcases were packed full of clothes and accessories. They only had one problem -- food. Tumi ordered pans of jollof rice and fried rice with chicken and croaker fish. They could keep it in the refrigerator to be warmed up whenever they were ready to eat. She also made some "amala" with "ewedu" soup and some goat meat stew that she took to them. That solved the food problem. With that done, she was able to pay attention to putting the finishing touches to the wedding program.

She had to make some calls to be sure the reception hall was in order. She was waiting for her daughter's reordered dress. She had to check on the lady contracted to do her friends' headgear and make-up. She had to be sure of how many people were interested so that she would be able to balance up the payment. She was excited that her sister was getting married. Inviting her over was the best.

She was grateful to God for this brilliant success! Everyone praised her for the support she gave to her sister. She was glad she was able to do it. She was delighted the change of environment brought about a positive difference in her life. Gratefulness cheered her heart that in a land where it could be difficult to find true love, her sister did not only find true love, but she was getting married and was also on the way to becoming a legal resident, in less than two years after she relocated. Such an awesome God!

Although they lived in different states and Carey was nursing a baby, Carey was the wedding planner.

She chose the bridal train wares, the fashion designer and the hall decorator. She wanted to use the same people she used for her wedding because they were excellent. A day was set aside for the designer to visit Yeni at her residence, and the bridal train crew reported there to take measurements. They were also able to see what style they would be wearing.

Contracting the food to a caterer was easy. Tasty Meals had a branch in Maryland. All she did was get the list of food to be served from the bride and groom, and she scheduled an appointment with the CEO of Tasty Meals in Houston, Texas. She was assured that all her branches made excellent meals and provided excellent services just like the headquarters. The bridal train wares were ready three weeks before the wedding. Carey made sure they were delivered. Everyone was astonished at the excellence in the product. There was no doubt that the decorators would do a good job as well; they were renowned for what they do. Since Carey was a nursing mother and did not intend to travel until a day before the wedding, she was always on the phone with Tumi. Carey connected her with the decorators and the caterers. By the time she arrived, everything was in place.

WEDDING BELLS

CHAPTER 13

The wedding was beautiful. It was well planned and colorful. Both families were well represented. The hall was decorated with lilac and cream colors. They had two events in one day. Yeni didn't want the wedding to be done on two separate days, so they chose to do both the traditional marriage and the church wedding on the same day. It was on the first Saturday in August and was a whole day's event. The traditional wedding was conducted between 9:00 a.m. and 11:00 a.m. The church wedding commenced at 1:00 p.m., and it ended at 3:00 p.m.

The bride and groom had two different outfits, each one representing a culture. The first outfit represented the bride's culture, Yoruba from the western part of Nigeria, while the other one represented the groom's culture, Igbo, from the eastern part of Nigeria.

The wedding reception followed immediately in the church hall downstairs at 4:00 p.m. The reception hall was beautiful. The décor featured lilac and cream colors. The tables were decorated with cream-colored table covers and lilac flower bouquets in the middle. The chairs had cream-colored covers with a lilac band in the middle. The tables were set entirely right with beautiful china ware and lilac-colored serviette papers. The cake table was a sight to see. The cream-colored table cover was overflowing, and on the center of the table was a stunning six-layer cream-colored cake decorated with purple, lilac and cream flowers. Surrounding the cake were candles, lighted as if paying homage to the cake. The walls were decorated with beautiful flowers. Yeni had to pinch herself to be sure she wasn't dreaming. She couldn't believe she was the bride. But when she saw smiling faces dashing toward her, her family giving her hugs and celebrating and, most of all, her handsome husband holding her hand and not letting it go, she was more than happy.

He held her close each time they had to stand and he deliberately showed her off to the crowd. The smiles and laughter came quickly. It was not easy for her to define the feeling because she had never been this happy. But she knew the feeling was that of joy, gratitude, and fulfillment. At last, she was married. She found her own man, at last! The life she had secretly hoped for even when she thought she would never love again had happened. Everyone who loved her rejoiced with her.

The honeymoon was sweet. The couple stayed in Paris for two weeks, and then the reality began. They were only back for two weeks before Ralph started asking for home-cooked meals. Yeni had been thanking her lucky stars because before their wedding, Ralph had shown preference for eating out rather than eating home-cooked food. She was not ready for the demand for home-cooked food. Yeni never really liked cooking. She had thought he was joking. The next morning, she made him an egg, sausage, and cheese sandwich and he declined the meal, saying he'd been eating the same for a long time; he wanted something different. She felt bad.

Her husband did not eat breakfast. What would she have ready for dinner? Lunch wouldn't be a problem because he usually ate lunch at work. Luckily for her, she could cook; she just didn't like cooking. She opened the cabinets in the kitchen and could barely find anything she could cook. She had to go shopping. She had gone to the African store with Tumi a couple of times, so she knew what to do. She went shopping, and by the time she got back, it was time for her afternoon appointment to do a client's hair. She had to go.

She got back an hour before Ralph, and she had barely started cooking when he walked in. He was starving, and he demanded food. She tried to explain how her day went and why food wasn't ready. Ralph listened to her explanation but did not utter a word. He ordered pizza for delivery, and he went in to take a shower while Yeni continued to sweat it out in the kitchen. She had to blend tomatoes with bell peppers, onions, and hot pepper. She had to cook the fresh turkey she had purchased, and she had to cook rice. It was too much to be done within the space of the time the pizza was delivered. He sat in the living room, eating his pizza with delight. By the time he was done, dinner was ready. He simply told her he was satisfied for the night and gestured that they walk into the room for a good night's rest. She was furious; she yelled at him.

"Why would you do this to me? You saw me laboring in the kitchen making dinner, and then you tell me you are full after I got done? This is unfair! I went to work like you did, and you still expect me to have food ready for you when you get back from work? Aren't you considerate?"

He did not utter a word. He went to bed and was snoring by the time she went into the room to challenge him with more angry words. She realized he was tired. He worked ten hours every day. He had been gone since 7:00 a.m. He had to drive one hour to work, and got off at 6:00 p.m. He usually arrived home around 7:00 p.m., depending on how hectic the traffic was.

She went back into the kitchen to clean up. She was so furious she couldn't eat. She packed the food into containers with lids and stored them in the refrigerator. She cleaned up the kitchen and was very tired by the time she retired to the room. She glanced at her husband's posture on the bed again, and she felt like spanking him like a baby. She decided to rest her aching knees from the hours of standing in the kitchen. She sat on the edge of the bed and leaned on a propped-up pillow. She was not ready to sleep until after a warm bath, but her body was so tired that she dozed off. She had been sleeping for more than an hour when Ralph turned around in his sleep. He saw her position on the bed and put her to sleep like a baby.

The next morning, she made breakfast. She made grits with boiled eggs, along with some strawberries and coffee. She packed him some lunch too. She packed the dinner he did not eat into clear containers with lids and had it neatly zipped up in a lunch bag. Also in the lunch bag was a small bowl of salad and an apple. She had a 2-liter bottle of water ready for him. She had it all on the dining table. It was apparent he wasn't expecting this luxury. He stood there, surprised. She watched him stare at the food, and she felt delighted when she saw the smile on his face. He invited her to join him at the table. They had breakfast together, for just ten minutes. He had enough time to apologize for his behavior the night before, and he was very appreciative of the lunch. She told him he would need a microwave to heat it up at work. That was not a problem. They had a microwave at work.

Ralph was able to boast about his wife's cooking at work. They had teased him about living a bachelor's life after marriage, and he realized they were right, so he had taken it out on his wife. Ralph was happy to show off. His male colleagues begged for some of his food but he only allowed them a taste.

Yeni, on the other hand, decided to work on her schedule. She only took walk-ins and appointments between the hours of 8:30 a.m. and 4:00 p.m. This gave her enough time to get home and prepare dinner. She enjoyed the mealtimes she had with her husband. It seemed to bring them closer together as they talked about work and other matters. He sometimes helped with dinner and cleanup. Some days, he would order food, and she didn't have to cook. They were a happy couple, who sometimes had problems, but were able to resolve them without bringing other people into the situation.

Yeni looked up some recipes from the eastern part of Nigeria and tried them out. She did very well with some of the dishes. Although they were both from Nigeria, they were from different parts of the country with different cultures. Yeni was from the west while Ralph's parents were from the east. He never really had the feel of the culture, except for what he had learned from his parents and their circle of friends in America. He had only visited the country four times in his entire life. He was, however, familiar with some of the dishes because his mom was always making them. He was glad his wife was willing to learn. Not that he really demanded it, but he was glad she did.

Yeni, on the other hand, didn't mind making meals for him because she realized it made him happy. She didn't mind adjusting her schedules either. It made her more organized and gave her an awareness that she was a responsible woman. She was still enjoying this feeling and struggling to like "cooking" when she discovered she was pregnant.

That was it! Ralph took over. The smell of food was too much for her first three months. She threw up a lot and had to be on bed rest for weeks. She survived it. Her second trimester was much better. She was stronger because she ate better, and the nausea drastically reduced. How happy the couple were! It was not easy for her to realize that she was becoming more responsible. With a baby on the way, she had more to do.

THE CAT IS OUT OF THE BAG

CHAPTER 14

Carey looked at her sleeping baby and smiled. Justin was a handsome baby. He looked so much like his dad; she only prayed that he wouldn't be a schemer like him. By now, she was sure Tosin was cheating on her. She was so desperate to know who he was with. On second thought, she said to herself, "What difference would it make?"

Well, what would she do if she caught him red-handed? She might file for a divorce, or just be separated from him. The thought of him touching another woman was very disturbing. She thought of confronting him with her conviction, but what if she was wrong? She would have to apologize to him. She would wait until she caught him red-handed...but when would that be? Her thoughts went wild for a while until she fell asleep beside her baby.

When she woke up, her head was lighter. She decided to put some things in order before the baby woke up. She gathered the baby's dirty clothes for handwashing. Baby detergent and softener would do the magic.

She was almost done when she heard him cry. She quickly rinsed off her hands and went to pick him up. There was no doubt about what he wanted; the enthusiasm for breast milk was very intense. Carey smiled as she watched her baby suck happily. Being a baby was the most innocent age a human being could be, she thought. Who could ever say this little baby has sinned? No heavy thoughts -- all they think about and ask for is food, and they will surely get it. The adult runs around to make sure babies are safe and fed while the baby enjoys it all. How she wished she was still a baby. The thoughts that had been haunting her for weeks would have been nothing.

The more she thought about it, the more convinced she became that he was cheating on her. Enough of being in the dark -- she wanted to catch him red-handed. Her convictions had better be wrong or else...what? She would leave him. Those were her words to Yeni before the wedding. She had confided in her friend that she was sure Tosin was cheating on her. Yeni wasn't sure of what to believe when her friend shared those thoughts with her, not until she saw him with Susan on her trip to New York with Ralph.

It was two months after their wedding and Ralph had to go to New York on a business trip. He took his wife with him. They lodged in a hotel where Yeni stayed whenever he went for the meetings, and they dined out every night throughout their stay. On their last night in New York City, they went out dining as usual, and she saw Tosin walk in, holding a child. He was with a lady she later recognized as Susan. She followed them with her eyes until they were seated. She stared so hard at the couple and finally decided to walk up to them. She didn't do it until they had placed their order. They were sipping their drinks and holding hands across the table when she decided to walk over, not without caution from Ralph. He thought she should leave them alone and pretend like she didn't see them. Yeni wouldn't hear of it.

"Carey is my best friend. I can never pretend I didn't see this," she said, getting angrier.

"I know, but take it easy," Ralph advised. "I'll walk you down there if you insist."

"Sure!" she said emphatically.

They walked to their table, and she said hello with a stone face. Tosin's expression was calm. He knew the end had come to his marriage.

"Hello, Tosin! How was work today?" Susan looked from Yeni to Tosin, demanding an explanation.

"Hello, Yeni! Susan, meet Yeni, Carey's best friend. Yeni, meet Susan," Tosin finally said in a very calm voice.

"Hmm… interesting," said Susan with realization.

"Will you explain to me what is going on here?" Yeni snarled.

"I owe you no explanation," Tosin replied.

"Or maybe you need no explanation. Tell your friend what you see, and you will take the burden off me," Susan said matter-of-factly.

"I have nothing to say to you," Yeni responded to Susan, "but to you, Tosin, you may owe me no explanation, but Carey deserves one. She does not deserve what you're doing to her; she trusted you and married you, and you would do this to her?" Ralph gently grabbed her by the waist and motioned her away from their table.

"Enjoy your meal," he said to the couple and walked his wife away from them. Yeni couldn't eat. She watched the couple from her table – eating, talking, and laughing. They occasionally chatted with the child in his highchair.

"They seemed happy together," Ralph said. He must have said something wrong because the look he got from Yeni was deadly.

"How could you say that?" she asked, furious.

"I said it cos it's true. You are ruining our night while they are enjoying theirs." Yeni stared at him for a long time. She was very furious. She got up quietly and was going to walk away, but she stopped herself as she remembered her promise to him to not be disrespectful -- not anymore.

"Can we leave now?" she asked calmly.

"No ma'am," he said with emphasis.

She stared at him again, this time with affection.

"Ralph, please," she pleaded.

"No!" Ralph insisted. "I will not let you ruin our night. We came here to have a nice time, and that is what we will do." She sat down reluctantly. They ordered food and were talking and eating when Tosin and Susan walked out of the door.

Yeni had a sleepless night. She was rattled by the conversation she had with Tosin and Susan. How could they do this? She was expecting a guilty plea, at least from Tosin. Oh, gracious God! Some men could be wicked! What audacity! Each time she remembered the way he had laced his fingers through Susan's on the dinner table, she shivered. And the child with them?

She glanced at her husband sleeping peacefully beside her. Could he ever cheat on her? She doubted it. The thought of it gave her the chills. Images of all kinds spiraled through her mind: when they met, how she gave him a hard time, his show and profession of love, and many more. He didn't seem like he could. All men are not the same; Ralph was different. Besides, she made sure she crossed her t's and dotted her i's during their courtship. She had left the rest to God.

Her thoughts went back to how she would handle the situation. Would telling her friend mean she was breaking up her family like Ralph suggested? If she didn't, what would happen to friendship dynamics and loyalties? Besides, Carey was more than a friend to her. Carey was like a sister and was her best friend.

She thought about the last conversation she had with her, and her heart galloped in her chest when she remembered how convinced Carey was about her husband cheating on her. That was a frightful conviction. Carey thus had a powerful gift of the Spirit she did not use before getting married to Tosin. Based on all she knew before their wedding, why on earth did she marry him? She wanted to stand in her face and say, "I warned you, but you wouldn't listen!" She really wanted to scream it in her face.

It was 2:00 a.m. when she finally dropped off to sleep. She hadn't slept for more than three hours when Ralph woke her. They had a flight to catch.

Hours after they landed back in Maryland, she picked up her phone to place a call to Carey but stopped in the process. Such news was better shared face to face. She would need to pay her a visit. But when? Ralph would not let her go visiting; she already knew that. Or, better still, she'd talk to Tumi about it. She had other issues to discuss with her anyway. Tumi would give her a bit of good advice about how to handle the situation. Yeni called Tumi to set the right time for her visit. She heaved a sigh of relief after she was sure she could talk to someone other than Ralph about it.

Yeni didn't have to wait for too long to discuss the issue with Carey. Carey called her and was crying on the phone. "Yeni, why didn't you tell me? You knew I was sure about it; you could have told me."

"I'm sorry," was her guilty response. "You need to take it easy on yourself…," Yeni tried to counsel but was cut short, "He's been cheating on me all along, and you want me to take it easy? How I wish I could kill him with my bare hands! Oh, how I hate him!" She then broke down and continued to cry. Yeni tried to calm her down but couldn't. Carey threw the phone against the wall, and it shattered into pieces.

Yeni was scared. She continued calling her phone, but it kept on going into voicemail. She was restless, yet grateful that the news did not come from her. She was not sure that she would have handled the situation better. This was terrible. She had never seen her friend in that state before, ever!

Then she thought about calling her on her house phone. She had never used it but was glad to have saved the number when she did. There was no response for the first three times she dialed, but when she dialed the fourth time, Carey answered the phone. She told her she was leaving town and that she shouldn't worry about her.

Yeni apologized for not telling her and added that she found out the night before, and she was looking for an appropriate time to tell her the news. According to Carey, Tosin told her himself. He didn't want her to hear it from Yeni. Carey decided to go out of town. She said she would be in touch.

MOTHER AND SON

CHAPTER 15

The street view from the 9th floor of the hotel room was beautiful. It was 9:00 p.m. on a summer night. She saw limousines driving past frequently. She did not have to wonder why because she was in Atlantic City, New Jersey -- a resort area with casinos in every corner. She'd probably walk in one day to see what they do. She wondered about how rich men play games with money. Some got richer and others poorer; such is life. Some people are already happy, and they get more comfortable; some are sad, and they get sadder. Hmm…, she was happy, then sorry, and she got more sorrowful. Was this the most disturbed she could be? But why? She threw the question into the wind. Why or how did she get herself into this mess? She thought about it, and she concluded that she had no one to blame but herself.

She thought about Yeni's words to her before she married Tosin. She was right; it was her decision. Yeni did everything to make her think twice about the marriage, but she was blindly in love. How could Tosin do this to her? He failed her! Now, her mom would say, "Did I not warn you?" She was glad Yeni didn't say it. Oh, Lord! What would she do now? Tears welled up and rolled down her cheeks. Her marriage was barely two years old, and it was over. She thought it was a dream. She pinched herself to wake up, but no, it was a reality. Then she thought about why God allowed it to happen. She was quick to answer her own question:

because she asked for it. God gave her real revelations. She had a series of them, yet she chose Tosin's words over God's words. It was a shame! A shame that she could discard God's Word and embrace man's words. She felt like screaming, but she turned around to look at her sleeping baby in the travel crib. She ran out of her room with a pillow to the living room, and she cried into the pillow. She cried continuously for about thirty minutes, sometimes softly, sometimes a little louder, but most times, tears just rolled down freely. She was exhausted. She walked to the room and saw her baby stir in his sleep. She walked to the bathroom to take a quick shower before he would wake up. The bath was refreshing. She didn't feel like eating anything.

She looked in the refrigerator, but it was empty. She was in a vacation home. She was supposed to do grocery shopping. She was happy when she found two bottles of water in the diaper bag. She drank one in a few gulps. Just then, Justin woke up. She picked him up and breastfed him. She always enjoyed breastfeeding. As the baby sucked, mother's and son's eyes locked, and they both smiled. If only for Justin, she must live. She must work hard and build a beautiful life. She was done with the marriage. Should she file for a divorce? With or without a divorce, she knew her marriage was over. She wanted her son to herself alone.

She would have to talk to a lawyer. Her daddy could help with that. She smiled at the thought of her daddy. He was the only one she thought would understand the situation she was in, probably because he had been cruel to a woman himself. His last words to her before the wedding were, "You told me he loves you and he treats you right; I believe you, but men change after the wedding. Either they love their wives more, or they realize they have married the wrong woman. The moment you realize he is maltreating you, run away from him because it will only get worse. Don't ever think of hanging in there."

After she had burped Justin, she gave him a bath and put on clean diapers and his cute pajamas. She put him in the stroller and decided to take a walk around the neighborhood. Hopefully, she would find a place to eat. She was starving after feeding the baby.

When she got back from the restaurant, Justin was ready to go back to sleep. She breastfed him again, and he fell asleep sucking. She gently laid him down and walked out of the room.

She turned the television on just to have something to capture her attention, but she couldn't concentrate on the show. She decided to turn her phone on. Her phone had been switched off for the past three days. The voice messages and text messages rushed in back to back. A lot of them were from Tosin but she was surprised he didn't say he wanted to see her. He was just sorry for what he did to her. He didn't say he loved her. Was she expecting to hear him say he loved her? He had probably realized that their marriage was a mistake just like she concluded. She deleted his messages. Some were from Yeni and her mother. She was sorry she had made them worried. Her dad also called. She felt terrible for causing anxiety, especially for her mom. She looked at the time and it was 11:00 p.m. That would be 5:00 a.m. in Nigeria. This was the best time to call her mom. Carey was glad she called because after having that conversation with her mom, she was relieved. Omolara had a wealth of experience dealing with men like Tosin and her father was one of them.

Next, she called Yeni. That was another comforting conversation. And then she called her dad. He was quick to send her more money for her upkeep until he found her a job.. After the three phone calls, she felt better and was able to sleep. When Justin woke up for his midnight suck, mother and son had eye contact again. She promised him never to give him up. He tightened his grip on her finger as if to say he believed her.

She gently laid him down in his temporary crib placed close to the side of her bed. She lay back in bed and sighed. She was tired of thinking about the present issue in her life. She decided to go on social media. The first thing she did was to block her husband from her timeline on Facebook, Instagram, and Twitter. She was going to stop visiting her social media pages for some time anyway. She decided to go on LinkedIn to while away the time. She was sure not to meet anyone close to her there. She had only a few friends there. She saw a new friend request, and she accepted it. She went on her new friends' page, and she read a story titled *Thelma*.

THELMA

Thelma sat in the chair in front of the big hospital building. She took another glance at the doctor's report in her hand, and her eyes welled up with tears. Could this report really be hers? Was she going to die? How in the world could this be true after she had suffered emotionally, physically, and financially, and was just getting back to a healthy life? She leaned back on the chair and took a deep breath.

She changed her attention to the people walking in and out of the hospital. Only God knows what illnesses brought them: some looking beautifully dressed in their office wear, some shabbily dressed, some just casually dressed. Their faces or outfits couldn't tell her what their illnesses were. Their countenance didn't reveal whether they were happy or sad. They just kept on moving.

Then she looked at herself. She was dressed casually, with her hair pulled up in a ponytail. She had on light makeup; she was beautiful. A lot of people had said that to her and Thelma took it as a compliment. She knew she was lovely. Each time she looked in the mirror, she saw her beauty. But for stressful days, there was stress in her look; she never liked herself then.

She wondered if she looked like the other people walking in and out of the hospital, or did she look worried. She probably looked worried. She tried to smile, but it didn't work. Then her phone vibrated in her purse, it was Keon. She didn't answer the call. How could she? The thought of leaving her children at their tender ages cut through her heart like a thunderbolt. Her eyes welled up with tears again, but this time, she let the tears roll down her face. She thought about what would happen to her children after her demise. Who would love them like she did? Who would talk to them when they needed advice? Who would take the younger ones to school? Who would feed them? Who would fill out their school forms, or sign authorization forms, or take them for doctor/dentist appointments? Who would play, laugh, and dine with them like she did? The thought was unbearable.

Then she realized she had to live. She had to fight this terrible disease and live-- not only for herself but for her children. How old was she anyway? She just turned 45, and she had two young children in kindergarten -- one was adopted and one was her biological child. How would she explain to Taylor and

Laura that she was leaving them forever, and for who? She had nobody but herself and her four children. The few friends they had were unreliable. She never had them when she needed them; she had no family.

At that point, she told herself she would rise and face the challenge. She would fight this disease; she would go for therapy; she would win. She would do anything but give up. If only for the sake of those beautiful words and little gifts she got from her children on special days like Mother's Day, words and gifts that expressed their hearts to her in their own way. She would fight this deadly disease; she would fight with therapy and prayers; she would not die. She wiped the tears from her face, stood up, straightened up her dress, and began to walk away with determination. "I am a cancer survivor," she said to herself.

Her phone rang again. It was Keon. "Happy Mother's Day, Mom!" he beamed through the phone.

"I guess you couldn't wait till Sunday," she said. "No, I couldn't. I wanted to be the first one to say you are the best mother in the world and that I love you from the depth of my heart to the soles of my feet."

Her eyes welled up with tears again but this time, they were tears of joy. "You just did, honey, and I love you more."

After reading the story, tears welled up in Carey's eyes. She looked at her sleeping baby, and she made another promise – to always be there for her son. If Thelma would not give up, why should she? Thelma single-handedly took care of her children. She was still thinking about them after she was diagnosed with cancer. Nothing compares to the love of a mother for her child. Then she remembered the scripture that says, "Even if the suckling mother would forget her child, God would not forget His own." Her faith was rekindled.

She also read a poem titled, *The Beauty in You*, on her new friend's page:
Where is your beauty?
Is it in the kinky elegant black hair?
Or on the glossy, shiny black skin?
Is it in the flawless makeover?
Or in the fabulous attire
That flaunts the beautiful curves
Of the well-built body?
No, it's probably in the shrewd and sparkling eyes
That speak volumes...

Aww! How can I forget mama's love?
That builds a healthy, loving, warm being?
Is that where your beauty lies?
Is it in the past memory that stings?
Or the past glory that lifts?
Or in the future?

I think beauty is in the new year
The new hope and original resolution
The new energy and new strength
The new life crying out to be embraced
And loved and cherished

It is full of endless gifts
Known and unknown
If you will only welcome it with vigor
You will find everlasting joy and happiness
As your inner beauty radiates.
Happy New Year!!!

That was a good poem. In place of a happy new year, Carey welcomed herself to the realm of a new life. Would she ever go back to Tosin?

She was taking a walk with her son in the stroller when two women walked up to her. One of them was tall and light-skinned; she looked like a black American. She was holding two boys of about the same age. The other one was dark-skinned; she knew her very well. The woman was her hairdresser. She was holding a beautiful girl. They stood in front of her blocking her way.

"Can I help you?" she asked, looking from one to the other.

"Yes, Carey," the light-skinned one replied, "you need to leave my man alone. I have birthed him two big boys. Carey, you didn't have to marry him to birth a child. What's your problem? Leave my baby father alone. I need him to pay these boys' bills."

Her hairdresser took over, "Carey, you're a fool. Why did you marry my baby father? He promised me marriage, and then you snatched him from me. I will never forgive you for that." She finished with tears in her eyes.

Carey looked from one to the other again before squeezing her way through them. She walked very fast, so fast that she didn't see someone walking up to her. She kept on looking backwards until she bumped into her. It was Susan with a stroller. She almost lost her balance as she struggled to keep the stroller steady. Susan was holding a baby over her shoulder. Susan eyed her wickedly and purposefully brushed through her as she walked away. Carey turned around to look at Susan. She stared at her until she was out of sight. With her head between her hands, she screamed in shame and agony. She woke up screaming. That was the beginning of the nightmares.

Some days they came even during an afternoon nap. It was usually different girls with children, claiming Tosin was their baby father or she saw Tosin hanging out with a girl. He was always happy in her dreams, and she was still sad. She sometimes dreaded sleep. Her imagination must have been repeating itself in her dreams. What would she do? She thought about seeing a psychologist. She could find one on Google. The problem with that was she did not like discussing Tosin with anyone. The more reason she kept to herself. Talking about it was so painful. She knew prayer would help but didn't want to do it. How would she start? Lord, I am sorry? Jesus, I have been wronged; please fight for me? God save my marriage, let him love me? I have broken up with my husband take these nightmares away? I pray for grace to keep my marriage? Help me, Lord, through the divorce process?

She didn't want to pray. But something stood out of the possible prayer lines that ran through her head: "grace."

She knelt to pray.

She broke down in tears. "Lord, I have come to you. Please help me. I am helpless. I have run away from people who could give me support, but I cannot run from you. Look through me, let your light shine through me and help me out of my depression. Lord, I am sorry... I need your grace to go through this challenging time for..."

She fell asleep praying and crying on her knees, laying her head on the bed for support. It was a quick nap. She woke up with a start and she felt better. She hoped the nightmares would stop, but they didn't.

Omolara's phone call came through one morning. She was thankful to God that her daughter answered the phone this time. She did not talk about Tosin. She gave some news about her siblings and a party they all attended the weekend before. It was a talk-of-the-town burial ceremony of a renowned politician. They talked about the display of wealth and the arrogance of the politician. They spoke briefly about corrupt politicians and the havoc their action brings on society. Then she asked her: "How are you coping, Carey? Are you okay?"

For the first time since she absconded, she replied, "No Mom, I am not okay."

"What is the problem, my dear?"

"I have been having nightmares. I have not had a sound sleep in a long time."

"What are the nightmares about?"

"I see these ladies telling me Tosin is their baby father."

"Hmm..." Omolara sighed heavily, "you have those nightmares because of what you think about during the day. What comes up constantly in your mind shows up in your dream. You probably think he sleeps with every woman he sees. No, I don't think that's what he does. I think he made a mistake. He has known Susan for a long time. He probably bumped into her, and the old feelings stirred up. He couldn't control himself, and the affair picked up from where it stopped."

"Okay Mom, on whose side are you? Why are you trying to justify his actions?"

"I am sorry, my dear, if it sounds like I am justifying his action. That's not what I want it to sound like. I only wanted to paint a picture of what I think happened. You will have to forgive him anyway. He was wrong, and he has realized his mistakes. You are his wife till death do you part. He is your responsibility. You have to pray for him and give him advice that will keep him away from other women."

"I don't understand you, Mom; you were always against him. Where is the sudden change of attitude toward him coming from?" Carey asked.

"I would never pray for any of my children to have a broken home. Whatever happens, I will always try to think of a solution to whatever the problem is. Besides, he called me," Omolara said. "He explained to me everything that happened. He said he was sorry. I could sense the remorse in his voice. I think Susan is the problem..."

"Susan is not the problem. Tosin is. He should have married her, not me."

"He chose you over her. You knew he had a choice, and so did you have an opportunity. You chose him despite his weakness and you will have to forgive him, if only for the sake of your child. You want him to grow up knowing his father, don't you?

"He doesn't have to, as long as he knows who his father is. I can be a single mom."

"That's the point young girls and women miss. You should ask me; I have been there. Being a single mother is not a bed of roses. If you have a home, you keep it."

"Ok Mom, I have to go now. I need to take a bath before Justin wakes up. I see him stirring in his sleep."

"Please sprinkle him with kisses for me when he wakes up. It's good you're talking about your worries. It will keep your mind free. Call soon, okay? You don't have to take my advice, but you can listen, and you can argue with me."

"Alright, Mom, I'll call you tomorrow. Bye."

The more she talked about it, the more relief she felt. She also had a long discussion with Yeni. Her nightmares gradually faded way. She was still not comfortable in the place of prayer. She felt guilty each time she prayed. When she discussed this with her mom, Omolara told her she had no reason to be guilty. She did nothing wrong, Tosin did. All she needed to do was forgive him. She opened up to her mom about how badly she hurt that Tosin did not just have an affair but had a baby with his ex. That baby part hurt the most. Susan could see him anytime, even show up at unwanted times. All she had to do was pull the stunt about her child. She had lost hope in her marriage. She believed it was over in less than two years from when it started.

Her mom kept on encouraging her. Mom did not want her child to end up like her. Her men left her high and dry, but hers was returning and begging for forgiveness. He wasn't even married to the other girl; she was a mere girlfriend, and a nobody too! Carey scolded her about calling people a nobody. Everyone is somebody, no matter their social status.

Omolara's men deserted her and chose other women over her. If they had come back, asking for forgiveness and were never married to other women, she would have taken them back. Building a home should be every woman's pride. Carey promised to think about her mom's advice.

Truthfully, she didn't know what to do.

A NEED FOR SUPPORT

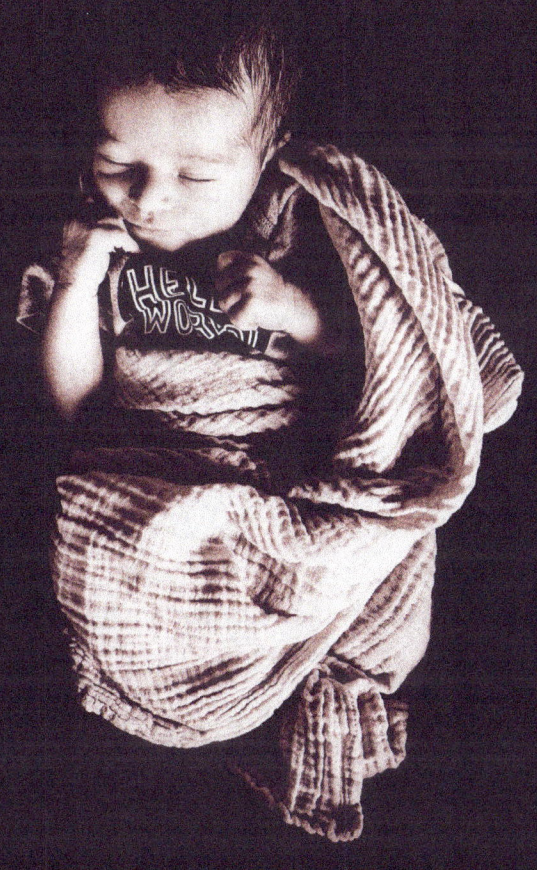

Tosin hadn't called or texted in the last five days since he told his wife about their love affair. Was this not a pattern? He met Carey, reduced his frequent visits to her and eventually left her when Carey threatened to leave him because of her. Was this not a repeated pattern? What would become of her and the baby? Susan wondered. She had been so comfortable making Tosin her source of livelihood. It made a lot of sense to her that her baby father was very responsible for footing her bills, including the baby's bills. But what would she do now? She didn't want to call him; she had decided to wait for his call or at least a text message.

She walked up to the window and looked at the streets of New York. It was a Friday morning, and the road was busy as usual, as everyone was trying to make it to work. She could get a job, take care of her baby and move on with her life. She didn't have to be heartbroken; she'd been there before. She had to be strong for the sake of her child. After all, life continues with or without a baby father. There were many heartbroken single mothers out there struggling to keep spirit and soul together, and most of them were doing very well. She could be one of them.

What job would she do? She had to find her people around here. She had to stop staying indoors all the time; she needed to go out and meet people. Then she remembered she had met a lady at the store who had wanted to be her friend. They exchanged phone numbers, but Susan never returned her numerous messages. She decided to start from there. She read one of her WhatsApp messages, and she sent her one. That was the beginning of their friendship. For a couple of days, they were exchanging friendly messages until they went beyond chatting to calling each other. Finally, Susan was introduced to the circle of her friends. Lola seemed to be a nice person.

She introduced her to another friend who gave her her first job. Within two weeks of Tosin deserting her, she got a job at an African food restaurant. She was also introduced to a grandma babysitter who wouldn't charge too much to keep her baby. Life was looking good. She was doing well without him. At the end of the month, she was surprised when she received a Zelle alert. Tosin had credited her account. She was happy and sad as she witnessed the same pattern repeating itself: satisfied that he was picking up his responsibility, and worried that she allowed herself to be used again. She could have continued with their agreement. She should have shut the door in his face the day he came back to her apartment. Why did she allow herself to be cheated again? She thought of revenge. She couldn't come up with anything. She thought of returning his money but realized that would be stupid. He had a responsibility to care for his son, his first son, too! She beat Carey to that. That was it. She felt she was in a sort of competition with Carey. She had always felt that way. That was the reason she found herself in this mess.

Love, courtship, or marriage shouldn't be a competition. Anytime it feels like it is, then a wise lady should break the relationship. She should have known that. Her mind went back to the last message she received from Tosin.

"Carey has left the house with our child. I do not know where to. I need some time to figure out what to do. Please bear with me."

For how long? The money he sent didn't seem to mean much. It only brought back memories of him being around her and the baby. He'd kept professing his love for her repeatedly, only for his wife to find out about them, and he was gone, again. His wife must not be coming back. She might divorce him. If she did, wouldn't that be a way for Susan to get married to Tosin? Wasn't that what she'd always wanted? Was that hope for her? Then she thought about Carey; she must have felt betrayed. She left her matrimonial home, what Susan was dying to have. That is an open space right there for her. She could contact Tosin and encourage him to come back to her. She could get pregnant again and have another child and that would ensure that Carey never came back to him. Her baby was one year already; she was ready to be pregnant again. With that conclusion, she sent Tosin a message.

He did not reply. She decided to pay him a visit. She would keep on pressing until she got what she wanted. She would not remain a loser.

She did not inform her Aunty Joy about her reunion with Tosin. She told her she was relocating to a new environment to start a new life. Joy tried to stop her, but it didn't work. She also asked her if this was concerning any new man in her life, but she told her it wasn't. This made it easy for her when Tosin disappeared again. The same weekend she decided to give Tosin a surprise visit was the same weekend aunty Joy visited her for the first time since she moved to New York. She was in town for a wedding program and wanted to visit Susan; she couldn't say no to her visit. Aunty Joy would probably be gone early the next morning, and she could still meet up with her afternoon flight. Joy stayed with her for the whole weekend. She discovered some men's clothing, and she asked questions. Susan had to spill the beans. Joy was furious. She slapped her hard across the face when she attempted to explain why she let him back into her life.

"You will never learn! Is he the only man in the world? Are you crazy? What is wrong with you?" Joy continued to raise her voice in anger and bitterness.

She forgot about the sleeping baby until the baby stirred in his sleep and started to cry. She stopped talking and patted the baby back to sleep. Susan broke down in tears, not from the pain she felt from the slap, but from the foolishness her aunt made her realize she had displayed. She cried all night while her aunt took care of the baby. Aunty Joy did not try to stop her from crying. She only told her that more tears were ahead of her if she continued to give him a chance. She had to confess to Joy that she was going to look for him that weekend. Joy had only one sentence for her. "Go and find him; win him over to you, and keep on fighting for him for the rest of your life. That sounds like a good life to you, not to me," she said with sarcasm. She correctly understood who Susan was, a woman who relied too much on a male figure to care for her financial needs. Nevertheless, she was willing to re-orient her.

She cried harder as Joy continued talking to her, "You can live your life without a man. You must find your feet and know who you are before you add another person to your life. Find a purpose. Be strong for you and your child. Men will find you when you are successful. You don't need him."

After Joy left, Susan cried a lot more. She realized Aunt Joy was right. Susan concluded she was chasing after a shadow. He had left them again! At first, he left them when she was carrying the child in her womb. He came back making promises to never leave her again. He just broke his promise. What could she do? Aunty Joy was right. She would forget him. It was not going to be easy, but she would do it gradually. She had to take the bull by the horns, concentrate on taking care of her son, and move on with her life. There were people with similar experiences who overcame their sorrow. She would not be left out; she would overcome hers also.

Lola came visiting, and she met her in a sorry state. She couldn't hide it anymore. Lola gave a short laugh when she finished her story. Susan sat up straight and looked at her. Lola sighed and leaned back in her chair. Suddenly she looked sad. Susan had never seen her with such a look; she was always lively and smiling. The look scared Susan.

"Your man left you with your child," Lola finally said, "mine left with my only son."

Susan wiped her tears and sat up straight. Lola told her a story of how she was married for two years without a child, and eventually, she had one. Lola was elated. The baby was her world. She had no idea that her husband had a different plan. He eloped with his mistress and her son after some months. For the past five years, she had not heard anything from him.

"I feel so empty without my son. I suffered emotionally before I had him. My mother-in-law was not patient at all. It was just two years into our marriage, and she was always all over me with curse words. I was sad because my family warned me against marrying him. My sisters invited me to church severally but I wouldn't go. My elder sister informed me about the danger of marrying a man without getting certified through prayers but I wouldn't listen because I was in love. My mom prayed and told me she had a scary revelation about him. She wanted me to take some time to think about what I was doing. I knew I was supposed to back out, but I decided to go ahead with the wedding. I had said to myself that prayers worked wonders. I would fast and pray, and the Lord would solve the problem. Here I am today, broken and lost. Well, I know it was all my fault. He was shady in his behavior.

Susan was at a loss for words. That was deep. She had never heard or read of a story like that. That was way deeper than her problem.

"What have you been doing about getting your son back?" Susan asked

"I did everything," she answered. "I went to the police, I paid investigators, I went to the media...what did I not do? His family denied knowing anything about his disappearance. Some of his family members were detained but later released. One of my investigators found out that he went to Germany under a different name with a lady. I have tried several times to get a visa to Germany but to no avail. But I should have something soon with my new agent."

"Do you have his address?" Susan asked.

"No, I do not. But I trust in God to find my son for me," she said.

Susan went into the room to check on her son. He was playing with a toy boat. She smiled at him and heaved a sigh of relief. "I have no problems," she said under her breath, and with the words, her troubles seemed to vanish.

COPING WITH THE CHALLENGES

Today was one of those days Yeni couldn't keep up with her clients. She woke up throwing up non-stop. Ralph almost didn't make it to work, but she encouraged him to go. He went late. The nausea was extreme, and the constant vomit made her very weak. She tossed and turned in bed until she was too frustrated to know what to do. She fell asleep and woke up 45 minutes later, feeling hungry. How in the world could you be hungry if you have no appetite? She dragged herself out of bed and to the kitchen. She saw a cold bottle of iced tea that appealed to her sense of taste. All she had to do was brush her teeth; she could smell her breath without opening her mouth. She had vomited so many times that she had terrible bad breath.

She was slowly sipping her iced tea and biting through a pack of saltine crackers when Tumi's call came through. Oh, gosh! She was supposed to be visiting her later! She answered the phone, and it was easy for Tumi to detect she wasn't feeling well. She was paying her a visit immediately. Tumi was off work since it was the beginning of the summer. She was pleased to see her sister, and she got ready to prepare some food to be kept in the fridge for the couple's consumption for the next couple of days. She was going to make some spinach soup with semolina. She also planned to make some stew with smoked turkey.

She thought cooking white rice wouldn't be too much for Yeni to do.

Tumi was impressed that Yeni had so much foodstuffs in the kitchen, knowing well she wasn't the kitchen type. That brought about the chat. Yeni had to explain her challenge with Ralph and why she had to shop and cook. And then, she asked Tumi about how she'd been able to cope with marriage, husband, children, and families simultaneously.

"It has not been easy, but it's been worth it," Tumi said. "I got used to cooking and taking care of the house. What I wasn't ready for was combining that with caring for children. Not that I don't love my family," she continued, "far from it. In fact, my driving force is the love I have for them. I realized that there was no help, and there would be no help. Hubby usually helps, but when the support is not consistent, and I'm not able to assign a duty to him, everything falls back on me. Waiting on him to help used to be very frustrating, and I was gradually becoming a nagging woman.

"I can remember taking a day off work and lying on my bed to cry out of frustration. I was a working wife and a mother; keeping up with my responsibilities wasn't easy. And I felt like I had failed because I noticed that there was a distance between my husband and me as a result of my constant nagging. I thought I was justified for being angry because I felt he wasn't helping like he should. He would get home from work, grab something from the fridge, and relax on the sofa, watching TV. I would get back from work and have so much to do: cleaning, cooking, caring for the baby and all, and I would be frustrated. After crying that day, I decided to do what he always said, "You don't have to do anything if you're tired."

"I called him to pick up our child from daycare cos I had to stop at the store, which he happily did. When I got back, they were both having fun, munching snacks, and watching TV. His diaper changing technique was horrible. He had the diaper backward, but he did it. I said I was too tired to cook. He looked through the stuff I bought from the store and was comfortable making a sandwich and pouring a cup of beverage. That was my breakthrough. He never complains when I get too tired to do anything cos he knows I'm not lazy. I usually cook and leave food in the fridge, and he's able to get it whenever he wants to, and that has worked for us. The nagging didn't do anything but tore us apart.

"I would advise you to be very patient and be considerate. Most men do not have the upbringing that requires them to give excellent housekeeping support to their wives. Appreciate the little your husband can do and ask for help when you need it.

Always remember to care for yourself as you care for your home."

By the time Tumi concluded, Yeni was already lost in her narration. She had, however, learned a lot from it. Then she said something about Carey. She told her sister what had just happened. Tumi said there must have been a glitch in their relationship before he could give another woman a chance. She went further to say that young couples needed to get things right. The first few months and years may not be too smooth because both parties are just getting to know each other. One thing that must not be lost is communication. "I almost lost my husband through nagging," Tumi said.

"Don't say that, sis," Yeni said. "Tosin was wrong no matter how you look at it. Why are women blamed when their homes fall apart? She wasn't the one cheating; it was the man. She didn't know how it happened."

"I am a woman and would never pray that such should happen to me, but I am saying we can hold our homes together through prayers, patience, and the wisdom to understand our husbands and give them what they want. I don't want you to keep on blaming Tosin without looking at this issue critically," Tumi concluded.

"OK, sis," Yeni said, "if you would blame Carey, you should blame her for marrying him. The foundation wasn't right. There was handwriting on the wall suggesting that she should back out, but she went in with her eyes wide open. That, I blame her for. Tosin is a kind of man she would have to fight for continuously. He got what he wanted in her, but did she get what she wanted? Girls are usually comfortable when they know they are useful to men. I know a girl back in my university days who said she was the prayer warrior her fiancé needed. The boy would not call or visit her for days; he expected her to check on him. When I asked her if she was his mother, she said yes. She was supposed to care for him like she was his mother and pray for him against temptation. Was he doing the same for her? No! She had so much of the burden on herself, and he had none. They made it to the altar, but he never stayed home. She was still his prayer warrior. It was easy to tell that she wasn't happily married."

"Hmmm… the burdens women carry," Tumi commented.

"We all need the grace of God to keep our homes, but it's harder when a proper foundation is not laid. I can say this from my experience with Alan. Although I wasn't married to him, I spent those years secretly praying for him to have a change of mind and come back to me. I was praying to God to do everything and let me not be ashamed. Well, I was already ashamed because he left me pregnant. My prayers were unreasonable because he belonged to someone else. Now I realize that the one man in a girl's life is not the only man that can make her happy. Other men could make her happy. If there is a glitch in the relationship from the start, there is a need for proper assessment, spiritually and mentally. The emotions at that time need to be tied up."

"I agree with you," Tumi said, "marriage is a lifetime event. Before you walk into it, you need to be double sure. What do you think Carey will do?"

"I have no idea," Yeni replied dejectedly. "She said she was going out of town for a while. I shouldn't worry about her. She'll call me."

"With the child involved, I agree she needs some time to think about it."

"Big sis, I have a question for you. As a marriage committee member in your church, would you advise Carey to divorce her husband?"

"No, I would never advise anyone to divorce her husband; rather, I will say the Bible does not support divorce. I will say take some time to pray and follow the Holy Spirit's lead. Some marriages are worth the divorce, if you ask me. A lot of couples do not know what to do from the start."

"What do you tell them when they come for counseling?" Yeni asked.

"I am always truthful to them. I tell them it's not a bed of roses; you must put up a fight to make your marriage work. You are intentional in most of the things you do. Also, you need to have a goal or goals to look out for in your marriage. That way, frivolities will not catch your attention and lure you away from your focus."

"Interesting… that sounds like a bit of good advice."

They discussed other issues about dressing and looking good for yourself and for your man. Tumi promised to take her shopping soon, as the need for maternity wear arose. Tumi's presence was much needed. Yeni was able to eat and keep it down for hours. She left shortly before Ralph returned from work. He was more than grateful to Tumi for a visit, especially for the food. As he devoured the meal, she remembered what her sister said about an African man. "They are used to eating home-cooked meals and will always want it. No matter how well they eat in restaurants, well-cooked home meals are their favorite. Some will stick to a restaurant that cooks the food the way they want it. As a wife, you want to cook what your husband loves the way he wants it."

When Ralph arrived home from work, he said he was starving. She looked at him and smiled.

She said in her heart, "I have one key to a successful marriage; I will use it wisely. Now I need to unlock more doors. I pray for more keys."

Ralph finished eating and heaved a sigh of relief, "I was famished!"

They both laughed. He suggested Yeni take the whole week off. She agreed with him. She had called off her appointments for the week anyway. Roseline, her assistant, would be able to take some and the others were rescheduled. She was still making money that way, just not as much.

As she lay down on the bed beside her husband that night, she was hoping she would get some pillow talk. She was going to fill him in on some of the girl chat she had with Tumi, at least the part that included Carey. She must have been talking for about five minutes when she heard him snoring. She sighed. He must be exhausted. Those were the only days he snored in his sleep.

The next day was better. She was learning every day what her stomach could keep down and how slowly she had to eat to avoid a vomit. She paid particular attention to the temperature of food or drink and to the taste. She had to order groceries for delivery. She needed watermelon, oranges, and lemonade. Hopefully, she would vomit less. She was able to eat the watermelon. She had it cut in pieces and cooled in the refrigerator. She ate her cereal dry for breakfast. She couldn't keep milk down, so she avoided it. She was still exhausted from not eating enough, but she was much better. She slept a lot and did not like the rush of spit in her mouth. Tiny sips of lemonade and saltine crackers were able to keep her mouth dry. She lay around the house, sometimes in her bed or her room, and sometimes on the couch. She was either watching a movie or on social media.

She microwaved some of the food Tumi prepared the day before and ate a few swallows. She was cleaning up when a message popped up on her phone. It was an Instagram notification. Tosin posted one of their baby christening pictures with Carey and Justin in it. It was a beautiful picture. And he wrote a caption: What more could a man ask for...

Many of his friends responded with words like: "You're blessed, man!" "Beautiful family," "Congratulations!" "You're favored," "...nothing more, you have it all." Within a couple of hours, there were many likes on the post. The picture was beautiful. Yeni stared at it for a long time and back to back. "But why?" she asked Tosin, looking at his picture like he was there in person. "You knew you were blessed with her but why would you hurt her feelings that badly?"

The image of him lacing his fingers with Susan's came back to her, and she felt irritated. She tried to reach Carey again for the umpteenth time, and her phone was switched off. She left her a message. She said a quick prayer for her friend. She didn't know the right or wrong advice to give her. He did not just cheat on her. There was a baby outside of wedlock involved. How would she encourage Carey? Tell her the child did not exist? Or wish him dead? Or convince her that her husband had learned a lesson and would not cheat on her again? Was that true, though? Would he not do it again? Such a man cannot be trusted.

She texted her and encouraged her to put her trust in the Lord.

HER DECISION

CHAPTER 18

Looking at the heavy rain falling against her hotel window, she saw her marriage falling and being washed away through the rainstorm. It thundered, and she shuddered. It'd been three months since she left her home and Carey was still not sure of what to do. The uncertainty was killing her. She had listened to her parents' advice, pondered over it, but still couldn't decide.

Yeni had nothing to say; she only wanted her to make a rational decision after a lot of meditation. Her parents' advice contrasted, but sounded somewhat alike. It was absurd that her mom would want her to reconcile with her husband because she never wanted her to marry him in the first place. The idea of a woman staying married to her husband no matter the condition was not for her. It was ridiculous how mothers advise their daughters to stay with a man who maltreats them with various counts of abuse. Some women suffer physical burns and are scared to leave their spouses because of threats, not only from the man but also from family members who would be expected to give them support when they lose their men.

Some women find it hard to get away from abusive men because men are the only source of income they have. If Carey had no personal funds, she would not have been able to leave, at least not immediately. She was also blessed to have come from a wealthy home without which she would not have been able to live in the luxurious hotel she was in. She should thank her dad for that. Her mom's advice about sticking to her husband no matter what, was somewhat irritating to her. She had been betrayed and emotionally abused. How dare Tosin desecrate their wedding vows so soon? Does it mean she was no longer attractive to him? Or Susan was more beautiful? What did he want? Why didn't he marry her if she was preferred? These were unanswered questions that never ceased to come to her head. The more she thought and didn't have answers, the more she thought of staying away from him. Who knew? Susan might decide to kill her for him.

Carey's dad wanted her to take possession of the house. According to him, he bought the house as a gift for her, not for him. He shouldn't be living in it if she's not. "I need you to evict him from that house! I paid for it with my hard-earned money!" Those were his words. He made her understand that he wasn't sending her any more money to support her and her child until she made the decision to go back to her property.

Living at the hotel for three months had been very expensive. Carey's dad had been very supportive. She couldn't do it without his support. She checked her bank account for the umpteenth time and funds were running out fast. She had to go back home. Her survival depended on the basic needs of life: food, clothing, and shelter. With the house, one essential requirement would always be met. She needed her job back. She seemed to like the idea of a nanny for her son. She should be able to afford it with her dad's help. On second thought, he might not be willing to help. He would require her to let the baby's father pay for the baby's expenses. That she wouldn't like. Anything that would make her stay in contact with him was out of the question for her.

Thinking about contact with him, she would need to contact him to move out of the house before her arrival. She had not talked to him in three months. She had blocked his phone number and prevented him from her social media platforms. She did not answer any caller that was not saved on her phone. That way, she was sure of no contact from him. He sent text messages from an unknown number to apologize for his action, and he also demanded a chance to explain his feelings. She read the message, deleted it and blocked the number immediately. He had tried text messages from up to three different phone numbers, but she deleted and blocked those numbers also. She decided to go back home in two days. She booked her flight and started putting her belongings in order.

When she got home, he was at work. That gave her time to settle in. When he got back, he was surprised to see them. He went on his knees, begging for forgiveness. She had nothing to say than, "I need some space." He looked at her and dropped his head.

"Please forgive my foolishness," he pleaded with tears in his eyes. "I have missed you and Justin over the months. I promise you it will never happen again. I have stopped seeing her since the day I confessed everything to you. All I am asking for is a second chance."

"Don't you mean a third chance? I need some space," she said again, this time not as strong as before. He noticed the tinge of softness in her voice, and he decided to play along.

"Okay, I'll move my stuff to the visitor's room," he concluded with some light in his eyes.

"Until you find a place," she concluded.

"Okay," he said.

He moved most of his things out of their room to the visitor's room while she sat down, making phone calls. He tried to talk to her, but she eyed him and went into the room, slamming the door behind her.

Two weeks went by, and they continued living like tenants in the same house. They barely exchanged words. He usually greeted her, but she never responded. When he was in the house, she stayed in her room with the baby. When he was out, she had the whole house to herself. She had contacted her employer. She would resume work as soon as she found a nanny. On a fateful evening while she was in her room, he dared to knock on her door. She ignored the first two knocks. On the third knock, she decided to open the door. She had a what-do-you-want look on her face.

"I want to see my baby," he said quietly, trying to catch her eyes, but she looked past him. She hesitated, then she put the baby in his arms. He intentionally touched her, and she almost dropped the baby. His mission was accomplished. He had the baby for the rest of the evening. To her surprise, Justin did not cry; all she heard was giggles from dad and son.

Tosin's desperation to have his wife back increased when Susan returned the upkeep money he had sent to her for the month. She also sent him a text message:

"We don't need your money to survive."

He tried to call her, but her phone was switched off. The truth was that Susan changed her phone number, and she changed her bank. She moved into a one-bedroom apartment as opposed to a two-bedroom, and she was managing to survive with her meager earnings. Her actions were supposed to help her forget about Tosin. She got more involved with the church activities and people, and she moved on with her life. Gradually she permanently closed the door to her romance with Tosin.

Tosin tried reaching her repeatedly to no avail. On one of his trips to New York, he checked on her in their former apartment, but she was gone. He was worried for some time, but he got over it. This increased his desperation to get his wife back. On his way back from work one day, he was in deep thought. He was thinking about what Carey had said to him: she wanted him out of the house. Her words hit him like a rock. His mind was so disturbed that he ran a red light and was hit by an oncoming food truck. The accident was ghastly; three other vehicles were involved. He lost consciousness, went into a coma, and did not come back to consciousness until after three days in the hospital.

When he opened his eyes, Carey was there looking worried.

"Tosin..." she whispered with tears rolling down her cheeks. He tried to reach for her, but his hands were too heavy to move. He tried raising his head, but he couldn't. He felt a big flash of pain in his head, and he cried out. Carey pressed the bell to alert the nurse. She had to leave the room to allow him to be examined. She stayed outside his hospital room, crying softly. She silently prayed for him to live. He did. He was discharged from the hospital two weeks later and she had to skip going to work to care for him.

She had to feed him because both his arms still had bandages. One night after she had finished feeding him, he looked at her and said "Thank you" for the first time,

She replied, "You're welcome." That was a good sign for him. He pushed further, "Carey, I am sorry... for everything." She nodded as tears flooded her eyes. He reached for her, she moved closer, and she gave him a hug, bursting into tears. He couldn't really hug her like he wanted to, as his hands were in bandages. That was it and they were back together again.

Her mom was happy that she went back to her husband but her dad had mixed feelings. After the accident, Carey believed he was genuinely sorry. He would have died knowing she'd refused to forgive him. She was grateful for an opportunity to revive her home. She called it the restoration story. She was silently thankful to Susan for disappearing from their lives. She believed the worst was over in her marriage. Her time to shine had come.

EPILOGUE

Life is easy
Life is busy
On the bright side
Standing tall
Never to fall
On the tower of greatness
Radiating brightness
Blowing kisses
At the entrance of fortune
Never thinking of misfortune

Then you ask yourself
"Is this me?"
Looking radiant and calm
Nothing to trigger worries
Nothing to plant the seed of sorrow

Guess what?
Life is sweeter than honey
Because you are on the mountain top
You're above the obstacles

You have the key to success
You are in charge!

The moment you looked down
The attraction and glamour
The distraction and clamor
Got you involved
You went down one step
And quickly stepped back up
Then you sat on the fence
You did not hear the voice saying,
"It's not allowed in this game!"
You sat on the fence
For a long time
And then you took three steps downwards
It looked glamorous
Shining like the star
But not the star
You went further
And further, and further
At last! You reached the bottom of the mountain
How easy is it to climb up again?

Now you talk of faith
Now you speak of trials
Now you talk of fate
What other options do you have?

Life is difficult
When you're on the dark side

Bending down
Bending low
Under the hands of hardship
Hardship blowing kisses at you
You want to resist
You say, "I want kisses but not from you!"

How sad that could be!
How bitter that could be!
How hopeless that could be!
But you chose his kisses
The moment you looked down
But asked for an added embrace
When you let him in

Then you say
"I'm going back up there
I've been there before
I can get back up there."
Yes, you have been there
And can get back up there
How easy can that be?

Looking up from the bottom
Of the mountain
You can always see
That alpine rope
Waiting for you

If you can only look up!

And stretch out your hand
The alpine rope is there waiting to take you
Higher than you can ever be.

ACKNOWLEDGMENTS

My gratitude goes to God, the giver of life, and all gifts. I will forever sing your praises for being my source and my strength.

I am grateful to my husband for his love, support, and witty sayings. In his quiet ways, he inspires and encourages me. I will say yes, over and over again. Thanks for being my number one fan!

Thank you, Mom, for your prayers and words of encouragement. You're the world's best mom.

Aduke, I appreciate your reliable support. You mean a lot to me.

And to Pastor Dele Akanle, I appreciate your support. Your ministry has indeed blessed me, and I am grateful to God for the day He called you. Thank you for heeding His voice.

Special thanks to pastor Ojo Odagbodo and his family, for their love and support for my family. May God continue to increase your ministry.

To my siblings and in-laws, you all have added value to my life in your way. You have been a part of who I am today. I am grateful for your show of love.

To everyone who has read any of my works, published or unpublished, your reviews are fantastic and a thriving force for me. With the whole of my heart, I say thank you.